Solomon the Accountant

Edward M. Krauss

Other novels by Edward M. Krauss

A Story Of Bad

A murder mystery and a love story, intertwined
Contains no graphic violence or sex

Here On Moon

Betrayal, Divorce, Recovery
Contains no graphic violence or sex

Solomon the Accountant

ISBN: 978-1-945975-72-1

Published by EA Books Publishing a division of
Living Parables of Central Florida, Inc. a 501c3
EABooksPublishing.com

ACKNOWLEDGMENTS

The author wishes to thank and acknowledge the staffs and resources of the Library of the State of Ohio and the Columbus Metropolitan Library, Columbus, Ohio and the Toledo-Lucas County Public Library, Toledo, Ohio, without which assistance this novel would have been extremely difficult to complete.

DEDICATION

For Esther, who makes me happy every day, and who encouraged me to tell you this story.

and

In loving memory of my parents, Martin Irving Krauss and Evelyn Krauss.

CHAPTER ONE

Toledo, Ohio, 1962

C ome in, come in! I'm so glad we're finally able to get together, I've been wanting to tell you this story for so long, but you had to go to your cousin's bar mitzvah in Cleveland, then that wedding I had to go to in California, Redlands, who knew there was even such a place. What a schlep. But a fine wedding, the reception…. and we've both been so busy at work. But now here you are! Sit, sit! That's the most comfortable chair. You want some tea? Like they used to say, a glaz tea?

So, the story. The story about my nephew and his wife, Solomon and Molly, now already they have Rifka and Jefferson, nu, a Jewish Jefferson, these modern kids and their names. And already Molly has another twinkle in her eye, I'm thinking…. I really love that little family.

A Jewish Jefferson… names, it's interesting, maybe you don't know I'm one of five children. You ever wonder why I'm Emile? You might not think of Emile as a Jewish name, especially for a man born and raised in Toledo Ohio, but that's what it is. So you know we name children for those who have passed on… it honors them and keeps their blessed memory alive. Well, it's like that. I am named for my great-grandfather, a French-Canadian, whose family came from France and settled near Montreal.

I keep interrupting myself. Anyway, the story. Such a story, about a motorcycle and such sorrow and such joy and such love. Such a love. The tea is all right? Need lemon? No? A cookie maybe? No? OK, the story.

Toledo, Ohio, 1950

Solomon Wholman stood, made sure his tie and kipoh were straight, and walked out of the office, turning towards the reception area. He signed the guest book then walked into the parlor. He had been to funerals already in his young life, but always for people in the next generation or even beyond that, people at least sixty, even a few blessed to live into their nineties. But this was for a young man, so young, dead so soon. The room was full, two generations well represented, those the age of the deceased and Solomon, and their parents, people who watched the dead man grow up only to be so suddenly taken. The sorrow was like a great, gray weight, the furniture and walls in appropriate soft beige and sand colors, the men and women in dark blue and black, their shoulders rolled down in sorrow, the heads tipped forward, the voices soft. Solomon walked into the parlor, looked at the closed, plain pine box resting on a draped table, straight-backed chairs facing the casket and the small lectern next to it. He felt suddenly awkward, not recognizing anyone. Then he saw a familiar face, a young man, and walked over to him.

"Lenny? Solomon Wohlman. B'nai Brith softball, remember?"

They shook hands. In a soft, subdued voice Lenny said "Sure I remember. How you doing, Sol?" He paused just a moment, then said "You knew my cousin?"

"Uh, no, not really, it's more that I knew about him. I was nearby, so I thought I'd pay my respects. Don't really know the family, though."

"Doesn't matter. It's good of you to come. Thanks. And come join us for shiva, we are going to need lots of company for the whole week, that's for sure. This is a rough one, a rough one." He turned, indicated with a nod of his head, not his hands. There were five people seated against the wall, almost completely obscured by clusters of people and by a slowly moving line of visitors. "Sitting there, that's my aunt and uncle, his parents, Jack and Nancy Manion. They are in shock, of course, really suffering. And between them is Molly, his widow, married ten months. At the end, that's her parents, Mr. and Mrs. Polsky, Ruth and Isadore Polsky… everyone calls him Izzy. They live in Chicago, can you imagine the phone call? Can you imagine Molly had to call them and say come to Toledo to bury your son-in-law?" Tears filled his eyes. "Ten months ago I was dancing at his wedding and now I am at his funeral. I can't believe … I am standing here … doing this. And Molly! Poor Molly."

Solomon put his right hand on Lenny's shoulder, squeezed gently. "I'm really sorry about your loss, Lenny. I'll go speak to the family, and I'll see you at the house. We can talk some softball. And the Tigers, maybe Detroit can do it this year."

Lenny smiled a bit, wiped his tears away. "Sure. Thanks again for coming."

A few people had just arrived, and although it was almost time for the service the receiving line was still in front of the mourners, moving slowly. Solomon got in line, feeling the pressure on his chest, sighing, caught up in the crushing sorrow in the room. Everyone was talking softly as they moved through the line, and the sadness seemed so thick near the family that it was almost hard to breathe. He would shake the hands, get out of here, back to the company's tax problems. Maybe he would go sit shiva, probably not. This was too painful.

The bride, the wife of only ten months, was sitting between her mother and mother-in-law. The three women were dressed all in black, small black hats with veils. The men, the fathers, were dressed alike, dark suits, slightly rumpled, white shirts, one wearing a blue tie, the other a tie of gray and black. The men had their ties pulled tight, their collars buttoned, their faces grim. The women had faces with red eyes, sad mouths. Except when they looked at the person immediately before them their spines were bent, their heads now and then dipping down, crushed by a weight that might never lift. Such a picture.

As Solomon approached the man's parents, the Manions, Solomon could hear the people just ahead of him – "So sorry…May you be comforted among the mourners of Zion and Jerusalem…..Anything we can do…Such a shame…May He grant you strength in the days to come…" – and then it was Solomon's turn. First he came to the father, Jack Manion, and Solomon bent over and said "I'm so very sorry" getting a firm handshake from a strong, work-roughened hand. He moved next to the mother and repeated the same words. To his surprise he felt tears starting to form; although these were strangers the sorrow was contagious. Nancy Manion looked at him a moment, took his hand in a brief shake, said "Thank you." Solomon moved a bit to be in front of the widow. She did not seem to see him, although she raised her face a bit her eyes were unfocused, as red as possible, tears spilling.

She was wonderfully beautiful.

Solomon almost gasped, stunned for a tiny moment. By the time her unfocused eyes met his he was again completely sober. Molly Manion blindly lifted her right hand, and he barely, gently touched it, lightly holding her fingers more than her hand. He softly said "I am so sorry." Molly barely nodded her head, looking at him without focus, with no light in her eyes. Solomon slowly opened his hand and took a step to be in front of her mother. "Mrs. Polsky, I am so very sorry for your loss." She took his hand, held it, patted it gently with her other hand. "Thank you for being here." Finally, her father. They shook hands.

"I am so sorry, Sir."

"Thank you. Thank you for coming."

***

Solomon reflected he had not started out that day expecting to be part of such heartbreak. In fact, it was a beautiful day in early summer when he turned his four-door 1942 Chevrolet Fleetline Sportmaster into the driveway of the Wickstein-Abramson — Zimmer Funeral Home on Jefferson Avenue. As usual, he was wearing a dark suit. He had a young face, looked younger than his twenty-five years, and he thought the dark suits would help people feel comfortable with him as their accountant, watching over their money. Always a white shirt. Always a dark tie.

A few other cars were pulling in at the same time, the last of the visitors, the small parking lot already almost full of Chevrolets and Fords, Packards, DeSotos, Dodges. The only Cadillacs were those of the funeral home, the limousine for the family and the hearse, their motors idling, waiting, about ten cars lined up behind. Halfway up the driveway a member of the funeral staff stopped the car in front of Solomon's, spoke briefly to the driver, then pointed and the car moved slowly to the back of the line. Solomon let out the clutch, the car rolling forward.

"Sir, are you going to the cemetery?"

"I'm sorry, I'm here to see your bookkeeper, business meeting. Where should I park?"

"May I ask you go around the far side of the building, just past the service doors? I'm sorry, but we need to keep the driveway open, not get anyone blocked in."

"Of course. Thank you."

Solomon moved his car gently around the arriving cars and the people getting out of them, noticing how many young people there were, people his age. He got to the far side of the building, parking close so as to leave as much maneuvering space as possible for the funeral procession. He picked up his briefcase from the seat next to him, got out and tried the building's service door. It was open. He reached in his pocket, took out a black kipoh and put it on, then entered the building through the service door, choosing not to mix with the mourners. He walked down a small corridor and turned into a business office.

Sheila Guytzen looked up from her paperwork. She was a woman with thinning red hair and a gently softening frame. Every day of her life she wore a Star of David on a necklace, a wedding ring, and several bracelets. On her desk were pictures of her with a man her age, with her grown children, and a few baby pictures. A nameplate on her desk said SHEILA GUYTZEN, *Bookkeeper and Chief Worrier.*

"Solomon, mine accountant, how glad I am to see you." She reached over and picked up a small stack of letters bound with a red rubber band. "I need you should unscramble this mess, the state wants more payroll withholding. I think they are farmisht beyond help, but maybe you can make some sense of this."

"That's why I'm here, Sheila. We will straighten out the state."

"I admire your optimism. Such a bunch of nudnics. So how is your mother?"

"Very well, thank you. And Bob? And your children and grandchildren?"

"All fine, all just fine, kineahora, knock wood." Sheila knocked hard on her large wooden desk three times. She pointed to a picture. "This one, Beverly's Amelia, mine Amy, she just turned one and suddenly she runs everywhere, I have to follow after like a protecting angel, she is into everything."

"You don't mind so much being a protecting angel."

Sheila smiled proudly. "I don't mind so much. So, you ready to start? You can use Stanley's desk."

Solomon took the government letters from Sheila, put them on the adjoining desk, put his briefcase on the floor next to it. "Sheila, who is the funeral for? There are so many young people......"

Sheila got a stricken look on her face, held both hands over her heart. "Oy, Solly, it's that poor boy, Darren Manion, you must have read about it, killed on his motorcycle, married not even a year and dead. His family is... I've seen a lot of funerals, a lot of grief, but these people are just ... I don't know what to call it......drowning. Drowning."

"Yes, I did read about it. Oy is right. Terrible, just terrible."

"You know, I tell my children, my grandchildren, watch out for strangers, make sure the car doors are locked, eat your spinach. So this means in addition I have to warn about motorcycles. I tell them 'You see, a young man with a new bride dead because he wants to ride a motorcycle like a hoodlum. Without a helmet yet. Better he should drive a car like a real person.' That goes for you too!"

Solomon held out his hands, his palms up toward her, a gesture of total surrender. "Never." He sat down, fussed with the papers a minute, then looked up. "Sheila, I must know some of the people in there, went to school with them or know their families... He was about my age, right? I have to go pay my respects. I'll be right back."

Sheila smiled her approval. "Such a good boy you are, Solomon. Your mother is proud."

***

When he saw the rabbi and cantor enter the parlor and start to greet a few people, Solomon moved toward the parlor entrance, not wanting to exit once the service was starting. He walked down the hall towards Sheila's office but stopped to wipe his eyes and blow his nose, then he stepped into her office. Sheila Guytzen looked up from her paperwork. Solomon just shook his head sadly, as did she. Then he took off his jacket, hung it on the clothes tree behind the door, and sat down to start wrestling with state tax withholding forms. He worked quickly and effectively, dealing with ledger sheets, payroll records, and tax returns from previous years. He was lost in the work until the sound of the prayer offered at such solemn moments began, the cantor with his clear voice singing *El Mal'e Rachamim* so as to break your heart in a million pieces. Solomon raised his head, listened, met Sheila's eyes, then they both shook their heads again and returned to their work.

CHAPTER TWO

S olomon Wohlman waited two days to visit the Manion's home. It was a wood frame two story house in a middle class neighborhood of similar houses, single-family and duplexes, most of them on small lots. In the back and side yards of almost all the houses were gardens yielding flowers, tomatoes, beans, cucumbers for pickling. A clean, well-tended neighborhood.

Solomon drove slowly up the street with many parked cars, unusual for a working day afternoon. He found a spot a half-block away and pulled in. He turned off the motor, then reached on the seat next to him, not for his briefcase but this time for a bottle of Manischewitz kosher wine, blackberry. Holding it cradled in his arms he shut the car door and walked to the sidewalk and toward the house. He saw a few others coming, a few going, everyone dressed appropriately, all the men in suits or sport coats, all the women in dresses. All those arriving were carrying something, a tray or a basket or a covered dish. Solomon hoped his being single would be sufficient excuse for bringing wine rather than something prepared at home. As did the others, Solomon did not knock or ring the bell but just quietly opened the front door and entered.

Inside the house were about twenty-five people, the conversation constant but in soft voices. All the mirrors were covered with cloths or small towels. As at the funeral home, the room was divided between people in their mid or late twenties and people fifty to sixty. Jack Manion was talking to three of the younger men, a small circle in the middle of the living room. Solomon looked around quickly but did not see Lenny and paused for a moment, feeling awkward. Still cradling the wine bottle he walked through an alcove into the dining room. As he did so he passed Molly sitting with four women in a small circle of chairs, but he gave only the briefest of glances and kept right on walking.

The dining room was full of food, the large rectangular table loaded with bread, challah, potatoes in several forms, brisket, corned beef, sliced turkey, several cheeses, tuna and lettuce salads. Also dill pickles - the real ones - olives, chopped liver, pickled herring, blintzes, sour cream, applesauce, iced tea, hot tea, coffee. Paper plates and plastic utensils were on the table along with silverware and china plates. On a side table were several wine bottles, Johnny Walker and Seagram's whiskeys. Solomon added his bottle to the table, wadding up the paper bag in his hand. He stepped into the kitchen where several women were washing dishes and being busy in the refrigerator and at the stove and with the large coffee urn borrowed from one of the synagogues. They looked at him with curiosity, he asked where he could throw the bag away, they showed him the trash container under the sink and returned to their chores.

Solomon went back to the dining room, trying not to look lost and uncomfortable. He hoped it wasn't obvious that he didn't know anyone in the house, was afraid of someone asking him why he had come. He really didn't know what he would say, didn't even know himself why he was there except that he had to see that face again, that wondrous, beautiful sad face. Solomon picked up a plate, stood uncertainly, then noticed a young man about his age also acting hesitant and unsure. The man had orange-red hair and freckles, and the phrase "map of Ireland" occurred to Solomon. Then the man spoke.

"Excuse me, Sir, are you Jewish?"

"Yes. And I'll bet you aren't... how can I help you?"

The Irishman looked greatly relieved. "Hey, thanks. Got some questions." He offered his large hand to shake, freckles and sandy hair on the back. "Murphy O'Geenan, Irish Catholic. I worked with Darren. What a mess, what a mess. I really liked him, we worked together the last six months. Gone. Just like that. Gone. You never know, do you? Was he a relative of yours?"

"No, just know the family." Solomon smiled. "Murphy, you're standing there with a world of food in front of you. Are your Jewish questions about this? You don't dig in soon you'll offend those ladies in the kitchen and everyone who brought a dish."

"Man am I glad to talk to you. Yeah, got two for a start. I know some Jewish people don't eat cheese with their meat, and I didn't want to offend everyone here by loading up with the wrong things."

"Not to worry. Some Jews keep kosher, and one of the rules is that you don't have meat and milk products at the same time, the same meal. Lots of other rules if you really want to keep kosher, do it right... but the rule you're referring to is that you either eat milk, cheese, butter, and fish, fish is eaten with milk meals... or beef or lamb, but not at the same meal. But other Jews don't follow that rule, and you probably know some eat pork, which is never kosher, while many Jews never touch pork products their whole lives." Solomon smiled again and made a broad sweeping gesture, indicating the food spread out before them. "So while I lecture you starve. The answer is that you aren't Jewish, so please feel free to build the sandwich of your dreams. Unless you dream of bacon...not available."

"OK, another one. China and silverware, or paper and plastic? Which and how come?"

Solomon was feeling a bit scholarly, a pleasant feeling, but he hoped the questions would stay within his scope of Judaic knowledge. "Same as the kosher rules. Kosher families have different utensils for meat dishes and milk dishes, different plates and silverware. Since I see only one set of dishes I'm assuming this family doesn't keep kosher, so they offer paper and plastic to those people who eat that way, who care. By the way, if these meats and cheeses came from Rosie's Deli, and I'll bet they did, they were sliced on separate and never interchanged machines. Same idea as the separate dishes."

Murphy smiled, tipped his head in thanks, picked up a china plate and began loading it with meat, tuna fish, salad, slices of cheese. "How about one more question?"

Solomon also began placing items on his plate, but not much. Although he had never kept kosher, wasn't raised that way, it suddenly seemed appropriate to not mix milk and meat on his plate, so he chose a bit of salad, two blintzes with sour cream, and three pieces of herring. "I might be pushing my luck, not a scholar and I didn't always pay attention in Sunday school, but go ahead."

Other guests came to the table, smiled or said hello, but since the two men were talking did not try to engage them in conversation. Murphy gestured toward the wall with his free hand. "Why are the mirrors covered? I'm guessing cause people shouldn't want to make themselves pretty at a time like this, shouldn't be vain."

Solomon nodded. They stood, picking at items on their plates as they talked. "Excellent guess. Yes, that is one of the most common reasons I have heard. But you have to remember that Judaism is almost six thousand years old, and there are bits and pieces of beliefs and practices and ceremonies that go way, way back in history. Besides vanity, I have also seen writings referring to spirits being attracted to mirrors, that the recently departed could be trapped in the reflection, or reach out to those still living, upsetting and distressing them… or mirror as metaphor, that at this time we should be looking inward at our own hearts and souls, not outward at our exteriors... I don't think anyone can say for sure why, for the first time, a family in mourning did this some hundreds or thousands of years ago."

At that moment a woman approached them. She looked at Solomon and said "Hi. I'm Susan Butler."

"Solomon Wohlman. Pleased to meet you."

"Murph and I worked with Darren. We couldn't get to the funeral, just couldn't, but we heard about this practice of family visiting and decided to come. I'm sorry, was he a relative of yours?"

"No, I didn't really know him, just know a relative, but it seemed right to come..." Susan nodded and turned to get a plate, and Solomon took advantage of this to break away; he wanted to eat the small amount he had taken and get out of there. "Nice meeting you Murphy, Susan. I'm sure the family appreciates your coming to honor your co-worker."

Murphy shook hands with him again. "Thanks, thanks for the good lessons."

Murphy and Susan resumed talking as she took some food, and Solomon moved away, got a cup of coffee and began looking for a chair. He saw one available but realized if he sat in it he would be sitting directly facing Molly, so he moved further into the living room and found a chair, sat and ate quickly and drank his coffee. Sitting there thoughts ran through his mind. He wondered if anyone else saw, realized, how lovely Molly was, or maybe they all saw and realized but only he was crude enough, uncouth enough, to think such thoughts at a time like this. He felt like a phony, a spy, sitting there eating their food and admiring the widow. He thought "Look on me sitting here eating their blintzes. With sour cream yet. What a meshugener I am!" He finished, took the plate and cup into the kitchen and thanked the ladies there, then returned to the living room where he approached the deceased's father.

"Mr. Manion, I'm Solomon Wohlman. I'm so sorry for your loss."

"Thank you. Yes, I remember you were at the funeral. Did you work with my son?"

"No, just ... well, actually, I know Lenny, your nephew. Played B'nai Brith softball with him. That's the connection."

"A good connection. Thank you for coming. And if you can, please come again. It helps to see all you young people in the house. It's like old times, when Darren always had a house full of friends. They were always welcome. You didn't come then, did you?"

"No, I didn't know... didn't have those same friends in high school, college. But my family was like that too, people could drop in, come visit any time. Kind of hard to be a rebel teenager when your parents are always feeding your friends."

"Yes, just like that. Nancy, my wife, she feels the same, always did, always welcomed them, probably baked a million brownies for Darren and his friends. Two million. She's lying down right now, pills for her nerves, they make her sleepy. So I mean it, please come again, she'd like to meet you."

"Thank you, I will."

"And not only to meet Nancy, but you see we have enough food for an army, and more keeps coming in. Everyone brings a dish!"

"It's so nice to have friends at a time like this, isn't it sir? Sitting shiva is a good thing we do for each other."

"It is, it is." Jack Manion paused a moment, and Solomon was just about to say goodbye when the older man asked "Would you like to hear a story about those days, about when Darren and his friends were still in high school?

"Of course, please."

"Actually it's more about Nancy, so you'll know why Darren brought friends home all the time, what kind of a home he had. New Years, it's his high school senior year, a bunch of them go out together, all these kids, mostly seniors, a few younger. Each one had a date, but they're all together because soon college, jobs, marriage, the gang breaking up. Some have cars, their parents' cars of course, they pile in, they go who knows where. All the parents are scared but they let the kids go after a lecture. A big lecture, but they let them take the cars and go. So they run out of energy and money around four in the morning, don't want to quit and go home like sensible people, so they do what? They come back here. So now six, maybe six-thirty in the morning, I'm sleeping like a log, had a few drinks and stayed up until one so I am out, out. But mothers never really sleep, do they? Nancy gets up, comes into this room, she sees there are kids everywhere, some asleep, some talking, a few smooching... You know what she says?"

Solomon couldn't help smiling. "What?"

"She says 'Anybody want breakfast?' That's how he was raised." He paused, looked down, then up again. "And now he's gone."

Solomon could only shake his head at the loss, the loss of a young man raised in such a fine home. They shook hands. "A sweet story. Thanks for sharing it... I look forward to talking with Mrs. Manion, maybe tomorrow."

"Good. Good, Solomon."

Turning away, Solomon made a slow circle of the room which brought him to the seated young women, Molly in the middle. They were speaking, so he hesitated, uncertain of what to do or say, standing awkwardly just outside the circle of chairs. After a moment Molly noticed him and paused in her conversation, looking at him with a question in her eyes. He saw that her eyes were still bloodshot but not so much as when he last saw her. She did not look away, her face neutral, passive. It was the first time she had really seen him and she wondered who this young man was.

Solomon took her glance as acceptance and moved toward her. Standing a respectful distance away, not reaching for a handshake, he glanced quickly at the others and said "Excuse me for interrupting." Then to Molly he said "My most sincere condolences. May He grant you peace."

Molly raised her hand, and Solomon moved a half-step closer, bent a bit and took her hand. "I don't remember your name. Are you one of my husband's friends?" After a brief hand-clasp she put her hands together in her lap, and he stood up straight again.

"No, actually I'm a friend of his cousin Lenny. I just was touched by, well, by us losing someone our age. I didn't know your husband, but he and I and those guys talking to your father-in-law, we're all the same age. We all should be around for years. It just isn't right, isn't fair. I'm really sorry."

"Thank you. Thank you for coming…?"

"Solomon. Solomon Wohlman. I'm an accountant."

A tiny smile crossed her lips, tiny and fleeting, straight to his heart. "Thank you, Solomon the accountant."

Solomon nodded, backed away, feeling like he had egg yolk dripping down his face. As quickly as he could without being obvious he got out of the house. Then, almost to his car, he slapped his forehead hard. Once in his car he started it up and pulled away, and as he turned the corner at the end of the block he said loudly to the steering wheel "What a smoothie. What a fine fellow I am. Go to the house where they are sitting shiva so I can check out the widow again, and end up with a commercial. Solomon the accountant. Solomon the widow hustling accountant. Oy. Double Oy." Solomon leaned forward, looked up through the windshield at the bright blue sky. "Sorry to offend. I trust you have a sense of humor, but I'll drive carefully just in case."

CHAPTER THREE

Herman Moskaivitch and Solomon Wohlman were lifelong friends, raised half a block from each other, Herman on Machen Street, Solomon on Warren, students together at Fulton Elementary, at Scott High School, at Hebrew School, and they listened to each other study their Torah portions for their Bar Mitzvahs.

Solomon followed a path straight from high school to Toledo University, earning his degree in accounting, then, following his two years of service, spent half a year with a small firm. At that point, with the dollars he had saved and a list of friends from high school and college, he went out on his own. Herman wandered a bit through high school, got his diploma but uncertain of a career, then worked part-time as a cab and truck driver while taking courses at the university. He left school, served his two years, and now he was dispatching at a trucking firm and getting a little concerned about doing only that for the rest of his life.

Herman and Solomon always knew that they would be each other's best men, come that day. Now in their mid-twenties, they both knew, in large part because their families often told them so, that it was time to get married already. So they sat in Herman's apartment on Robinwood, not far from the art museum, and talked, again, about women.

"So Solly, whatcha think's doing this weekend?"

"What are you asking me for? You're going to spend the weekend at Deb's, eating her mother's cooking, taking her father's money at penny-a-hundred gin rummy. They only put up with you because maybe someday you'll ask Deb to marry you. Someday. Maybe."

"Well, actually, we're kinda off…"

"What this time? Forget her birthday?"

"How good-a friends are we?"

Solomon indicated the bond of their friendship with an appropriate single-finger salute. "So this is a royal screw-up. You did forget her birthday."

"Crude but unfortunately highly appropriate gesture and choice of words. Deb and I were here and… about to share a moment… when suddenly I realized that I forgot… to be safe. To get a new supply of safety."

"Euphemisms till I could puke. OK, you forgot your rubbers, so you just kissed and went to the movies instead."

Herman got up from the brown and beige checked couch that he had bought at a closeout sale from a furniture store that seemed forever to be closing out. He walked over to the record player and put on a 78, a T-Bone Walker collection. Solomon waited.

Herman returned to the couch, listened a bit, then said "Deb in one of her supercharged fun-girl moods. She says let's do it anyway, roll the dice, she gets pregnant we'll just get married sooner than we planned."

"And you said 'That's my girl' No, you said 'Sure, why not?' No, you said…"

"Bite me."

"Oh, that's perfect, perfect!"

Now Herman raised a finger. "Not her putz-face, you!"

"So you want a go to the deli, get some pastrami and dills, belch garlic at the pretty girls? Maybe find you someone new."

"And first, I don't want anyone new. And second, I'm in the middle of a story here. Could we have a little polite listening, you could stop being an asshole for one minute?"

Solomon bowed his head and made a sweeping gesture of acceptance with his hand. "Please continue with this touching story of how you have again irritated the lovely Deborah Goldman, who everyone knows is far too good for you."

"Ignored. So she says let's take a chance, maybe we'll have to get married, and I didn't say anything. Nothing! Look how innocent I am!"

"Wait, wait… A lovely lady says to you that she would like to get married to you sooner instead of rather later and you say nothing?"

"Right! Innocent!"

Solomon got up from the soft chair he was sprawled in, walked over to Herman and rapped him once on top of his head. Standing over him, he said "Wrong! Guilty!" Another rap. "Twice guilty! Not only did you fail to make the proper response, but you also failed to make it immediately, instantly, as fast as words can be spoken…"

Herman looked up, rubbed his head where the raps had been received, then sighed and looked down. "Yeah, I know, I shoulda told her that was fine with me, let's have a baby, let's get married…"

Solomon sat down next to him on the couch. "Married then baby, or no more food from the mother… and no more pennies from the father. So what happened next?"

"What happened next was the temperature in the room dropped fifty degrees in five seconds and like that I'm alone by the telephone."

"She split?"

"Never knew a woman could get dressed that fast. Gone. I'm trying to apologize and she's in her car and outahere. Home to mommy before I can get my fly zipped."

Solomon nodded slowly, wisely. "Flowers. Candy."

"You think I'm a shnook? Like I don't know women? Tried flowers and candy, went to the library to look up lovey quotes to write on the cards that went *with* the flowers and the candy. Nothing. Nada. Not even close. Ice-cold silence reigns."

"This is only a temporary setback...."

"I don't know...."

"Total bullshit. You trying to tell me you're giving up? Deb? Come-on, the light of your life, right?"

"She wants me to say it."

"You're the light of my life? Corny, but if she wants that...."

"It. The big it. The Biiiiiig it!"

Solomon leaned back, stroked where his beard would be if he didn't shave almost every day, believing people wanted to see their accountants clean shaven in addition to dressed conservatively. He spoke slowly, an old philosopher, as if trying to understand a deep mystery. "The big it...what could it be...not I love you, you've said that, I've heard you.....

"Solly, my man, 'I love you' is the small it. The big it is..."

The light bulb came on for the ancient thinker. "Will you marry me?"

"Almost. Actually the exact wording is 'Will you *please* marry me.'"

"Problem being...?"

"Oy. I need a little more time, that's all, just a little more time."

Now the wise philosopher dispensed judgment from on high in solemn tones.

"This is beyond Oy. Time has run out."

"Use it or lose it."

"A Jewish pig. No, not use it or lose it. Look, just go to her house, get down on a knee, either one, your choice, and say it. Just like you just did, same way..." Here Solomon switched to the mock-Yiddish accent and inflection they sometimes used with each other, with the sing-song qualities and Eastern European flavor. "Although… a tremble….. in the voice… vouldn't hoit."

Herman sat, stared down at his shoes a moment, then sighed and said without lifting his head "You're right."

"Perfect. Look, I'll drive you there, you can fly home on wings of love."

"And screw you too."

"Come-on, shine your shoes, put on a clean shirt and tie, and go ask Delectable Deborah to please please marry you."

"Maybe I need some pastrami to give me strength."

"Maybe you do, but first for five minutes you could be serious. You going to do it? You going to go propose to that fine lady before she finds someone better? Which by the way is such an easy thing to do."

"And the horse you rode in on. Yeah, gonna do it. I love her, don't think I could live without her. So I'll get up my courage and ask her. One of these days. Soon. Then you can get a date and we can double. Unless you've been rejected by every available woman in five states. What you think, could you get a date? You might even find one desperate enough to marry you."

"Not yet proposed and already trying to marry me off. Lecture on me about getting married after you ask Deb, OK? Of course, she may say no, being such a smart lady."

Herman leaned back in the couch, turned, moved his head from side to side as if trying to see something that was hidden, unclear. "I sense evasion. Something is up, and not what should be up. Talk to me, Solly. New woman in your life? Keeping secrets from Herman?"

"As a matter of fact, yeah, something cooking. Off to Rosie's. Pastrami and revelation."

"Wrong Bible."

"Wrong friend."

CHAPTER FOUR

A unt Rosie Cohen's Delicatessen on Ashland Avenue was a center point in Jewish life in Toledo in the years before the migration north and west toward Ottawa Hills and Sylvania. As a concession to modern business demands it was open Saturdays, closed only Mondays, but although open on the Sabbath everything inside was strictly Kosher, as certified by the Vaad Hakashrut. Long tubes of Hebrew National hard salami hung from the ceiling, brisket and rye bread and matzo ball soup was always available, every day, as was herring in wine sauce and herring in sour cream and regular corned beef, which meant somewhat fatty, and lean corned beef, and slaw and pickles and pickled tomatoes. As Solomon had told Murphy O'Geenan, separate slicing machines and knives, and other implements were used for the meats and the dairy products, never ever interchanged. The knives for cheese were marked with blue on the handle, those for meat with red. The aroma, for those raised to it, was the smell of heaven.

As usual, the deli was noisy, bustling. Rosie's was usually full or nearly so, with someone waiting for a table almost all day Sunday. This evening, a weekday, they were able to be seated right away, but not many tables or booths were empty. The two men were seated at a booth along the wall, approached after a bit by a waitress, short, thin, moving fast, in her mid-forties. She wore an shirtwaist dress of light yellow, a pencil stuck in her bun of hair twisted on top of her head, and was given to a New York affectation; that is, she believed people in delis wanted a brusque waitress who was all business, no humor. She slammed two water glasses down, magically not spilling a drop, then retrieved her pencil and stood with her pad, waiting, properly bored.

Without looking at the menu the friends both ordered pastrami on seeded rye, regular mustard, which meant yellow, side of slaw, Faygo black cherry. The drinks were brought to them first, bottles along with glasses half full of ice. Solomon lifted his bottle, tilted it slightly toward Herman who picked up his bottle and clinked it against the other. The ceremony completed, they poured their drinks and sat back. Solomon spoke first.

"Well, I have been on your case about Deb, totally right in every way, of course."

"Of course…"

"But now it's your turn. You'll never guess what I've done."

"So was that an invitation to a puzzle, or a lead-in to an exciting tale of adventures in accounting, like how you balanced the books in only nine hours? In other words, should I guess?"

"Nah. I'll just tell you." Solomon poured a little more in his glass, put the bottle down and lifted his drink, took a sip, put the glass back on the table. Herman waited patiently. "Herman old putz, do you believe in love at first sight? Do you think people can look at each other and know, right then know, that is their person?"

"Are we having a serious conversation? You know, just so I know if this is horseshit or not. You know."

"I'm in love. I'm so in love I can't think. I don't want to spend five minutes with anyone else."

"I almost think you mean this. You saw this girl and, what, now you are sold this is the mother of your children? One look? This is so un-accountant of you, I almost think you mean it."

"I mean it."

"Lucky you! Poor girl, but lucky you. When can I meet the mystery lady? No, when can we meet the mystery lady, cause I'm gonna propose any minute now. Yeah, well, maybe not any minute, but any day. Or week. Or month. Yeah, any month."

"Such conviction. Deb heard you right now she'd be long gone."

"Ducking, ducking. Repeating, he said, when can I meet the mystery lady?"

"Maybe I could point her out in a grocery store, or we could wait in the car like detectives and I could point as she walked by."

"There is a problem."

"There is a problem."

"She's not Jewish."

"She is Jewish."

Herman leaned back as far as the booth would allow, stroked his clean-shaven chin as if he had rabbinic whiskers, pursed his lips and gazed at the ceiling. "Come, my children, let us review.... let us study this puzzlement. I can meet her only in retail establishments, she is Jewish, but there is some problem...."

"She's in mourning."

"Oy. For her father."

Solomon sat, his hands wrapped around his glass of Faygo, looking at his dear, life-long friend.

"For her mother."

Still Solomon sat still.

"A brother, a sister...?"

At that moment the waitress appeared next to the booth. She slid stacked pastrami sandwiches, cut in half, with a large dill pickle in front of each of them, the slaw in small bowls balanced on the plates next to the pickles. "Ene-thin else?" she asked in her best New York imitation.

Both men said, almost as one, "No, thanks." Herman picked up a half sandwich and bending slightly forward, took an enormous bite of the meaty sandwich. Solomon sat as before, his eyes on Herman's face, the food untouched. Suddenly Herman's eyes opened wide, and he hurried to chew and swallow. "Her husband!"

In response, Solomon picked up his pickle and bit off one end with a snap. Then he picked up his sandwich and began eating.

"Could it be?"

Speaking around his bite of pastrami, Solomon said "Could it be what?"

"Accountant, does the books for wealthy elderly couple, old man dies, rich old woman covets young... well, certainly not a stud, but..."

"Young woman. Young widow."

"Still in mourning."

"Still in mourning."

"But ready to find someone new. Been ten, eleven months now, right?"

"Right about the ten. Wrong about the months."

"Weeks."

Again Solomon sat, looking, this time a sad, wistful look on his face.

"Not... days! Not an ten-day widow. You've fallen in love with a woman whose husband is dead not yet two weeks?"

As before, Solomon indicated yes by returning to his eating, eyes downcast.

"This is a sin!"

"No it's not."

"No it's not."

They spent some time eating. When they were almost finished Herman spoke again. "I assume this is one sided, it is all in your very strange brain. You haven't said anything to her, have you?

"Why did I choose such a num-nuts for my best friend? Of course not."

Herman finished his food, sat back. "OK, bubbila, tell me the story."

"You remember... you should remember, it just happened, big story about it... Darren Manion got killed on his motorcycle? It's his wife. She's his wife. Widow. Molly. Molly with the perfect face inside my soul."

"Yeah, got your soul. So what happened?"

"I'm at Wickstein's, got a tax problem to fix, as I get there people are gathering. They almost put me in the funeral procession. Anyway, so there I am, and I see all these young people our age coming for the ceremony, so I ask the bookkeeper who the funeral is for and she tells me it's for the man in the motorcycle accident. Well, I couldn't just start doing the books. It just got to me, death of a guy our age, so I had to go say something. Turns out I know a cousin of...of Darren's, Lenny Weitz, we played B'nai Brith softball together. Know him?"

"No."

"Not important. Anyway, I pay condolences, and I look in her eyes... no, I looked at her eyes, she was just blank, didn't see me or anything much, I guess... but I saw her dark eyes and beautiful face and like a hammer, like a punch in the gut I am so in love I can't stand it."

"I don't believe I'm hearing this. You mean it. You're serious."

"Very. Even a little scared, I guess."

Herman brightened, held up an index finger, arched his eyebrows. "I'll bet I know what you did."

"What did I did?"

"You went to the house. You went there under the guise of offering support, sitting shiva, when in fact you were scoping out the widow. Now that is a sin."

Solomon responded in defense. "I brought a bottle of wine."

"Oh we are so impressed. Oh that is so nice of you. Doesn't begin to balance the scales, schmuck, but nice."

"All three times I brought a bottle of wine. And some kosher chocolate candy imported all the way from Detroit even."

Herman's voice rose in pitch, almost a squeak. "Three times!"

"Shiva is a week, maybe you forgot."

"Lecture me not, sinner. Next Yom Kippur just stand all day, even during the sermon, you have so much to ask forgiveness for. Let us clarify… you don't know her, or her family, or his family, am I correct?"

"Aside from the cousin… no."

"OK, aside from a distant connection by way of Jewish softball you have no connection, but there you are. Three times."

Solomon delivered a brief lecture. "Sitting shiva is a week of offering comfort and support, keeping the family company while they deal with the grief."

"Thank you, rabbi. I know what shiva is about. I also know what you are about."

"I hardly spoke to her. I offered condolences, but never tried to talk to her, or to join in a conversation she was having. Really. She saw me, I shook her hand, said a few words. That's about it."

"Oy I feel like a detective getting the guilty guy to give up the story one piece at a time. Such a putz. I hear your little weasel word, I heard you say 'about.' Meaning…"

Solomon confessed "I told her I was an accountant. Sounded like a commercial. I almost dope slapped my forehead. Actually, I did dope-slap my forehead, but I waited until I was out of the house."

"So now what?"

Solomon shrugged, a large, sad gesture. "Now I guess I sit on my hands for a while, then ask her to marry me."

"Just like that? I can make a suggestion here? Maybe you should date once or twice before offering a proposal of marriage to your dope-slapped self. She has to wait a year to do anything social, right?"

"A year if one loses a parent. For a spouse it is sheloshim. I looked it up."

"Again the rabbi. Sheloshim?"

"Hebrew for thirty. Thirty days is the mourning period. Of course, that's only a rule, a minimum. For someone crying like she was, who knows how long 'til she wants to know from a date, let alone marriage."

Herman Moskaivitch looked at Solomon. "You're gone, aren't you?"

"Gone, all the way."

CHAPTER FIVE

T he pictures remained on the coffee table, on the mantle, in the bedroom. Pictures of Molly and Darren dating, smiling in the bright sun on a Michigan ski slope, hugging on a couch at a party surrounded by friends. And of course the wedding pictures, the bride in her white dress, making her dark hair and eyes even more powerful, electric. The groom in his tuxedo, a look on his face to melt your heart. The framed wedding invitation, just a year old, inviting all to the wedding of Molly Polsky and Darren Manion. Molly let her eyes brush over the pictures, the framed invitation, as she moved about the apartment, but she didn't look hard at them, didn't linger. She moved through the days in a numb state, staying awake some nights until almost dawn, others falling asleep from exhaustion before sunset.

The phone rang. Even as she picked it up Molly knew it was her mother.

"Hello?"

"Hello, Molly."

"I just felt it was you calling, Ma. Guess I know your ring."

"I shouldn't bother you just now?"

"No, Ma, it's fine. How's Dad?"

"At the store, of course."

"Of course." Molly sat on an ottoman in front of what had been Darren's favorite chair. She leaned forward, rubbed her forehead, sat hunched over.

"Molly, I want to say something, you shouldn't be mad at me."

"Mother, it's fine, I won't be mad. What?"

"Well, I didn't want I should be a bother on you while we were sitting shiva, and then we had to get home in a hurry, your father had to get back to the store. Always with the store. I tell him I don't want to be the richest widow in the synagogue, better he relaxes once in a while, so maybe he is a little poorer and lives a little longer. But about you. You want to come home, move back to Chicago?"

Molly answered at once, but with tenderness. "No, Ma, I don't. I love you and Dad, but I've got friends here, and a job, and I didn't want to... I don't want to jump into anything new or different. It feels good to keep up a routine, see the same faces... and I'm all grown up now... If I moved back in with you we'd make each other nuts in short order."

"What a thing to say."

"Mom, don't be offended, I didn't mean anything harsh, just that I'm grown, I've grown up, it wouldn't..."

"Mollia..."

"Mom, I just don't feel like moving and looking for an apartment, then looking for a job... and I have friends here, and I like the school, I work with nice people and the kids are fun, they make us all a little crazy sometimes but they're fun, and sweet... so I'm staying in Toledo and... and... just settling, calming down for a while. Please, please Ma, hok nit kain tchynik about this. I need to stay here, at least for a while."

There was just the briefest pause, in mother-daughter code it meant disappointment but acceptance.

"You'll come for visits."

Molly gave a brief, gentle laugh. "No, Ma, I'll never come for a visit. Never. Or, how about Thanksgiving..."

"Not until Thanksgiving?"

"Maybe before, maybe, but Thanksgiving is a promise, Hanukkah, too. I need my Mommy's latkes."

"And you can call."

"Yes, I can call. And you can call, and Dad. And write. I like letters, and you can keep them…. sit at the kitchen table and write me a letter. And I'll write. Let's write letters, we'll write, we'll call…"

"Good. We won't be strangers."

"No, we won't be strangers. Now call Dad and tell him I love him and that he should come home and spend less time in that store of his. Tell him he should take his wife for a walk, go to the deli, see a movie."

"Like talking to the wall……"

CHAPTER SIX

S olomon Wohlman sat at his desk in his small one-room office. The only decorations on the faded, off-white walls were his Bachelor's Degree from Toledo and his CPA certification. The office was all business; books, papers, an electric adding machine he bought from the army surplus store, its shell olive drab. There were two file cabinets with some files stacked on top and his somewhat battered second-hand desk chair, one desk lamp and one floor lamp. His chair was padded just a bit, and there was one guest chair, hard wood, from another surplus sale, a similar chair against the wall, available if needed for two visitors but currently serving as yet another storage device.

Solomon glanced at his watch, put down his pen and straightened the papers he was working on so he could place them neatly in a file, which he moved to the left side of his desk. He glanced at his watch again, got up and took his sport coat off the hook on the door, put it on and tightened his tie. He left the office, checked to make sure the door was locked, then went down a hallway and down one flight of stairs. The office was on the second floor of a building that contained a branch of Toledo Savings and Trust; he thought it seemed a good thing for an accountant to be in an office building with a bank branch on the first floor, a good business image. At the bottom of the stairs he exited into a small lobby that opened both to the stairs and to the bank lobby. There was also a small elevator for the five-story building, and a directory of the occupants, mostly attorneys, doctors, insurance agents, Solomon and another accountant, a three-person firm. He walked out of the lobby, turned left and walked briskly past several office buildings, lunch shops, a shoe store. He came to another small office building and stopped, leaned against the wall near the revolving doors.

It was shortly past five, and people began streaming out as the offices closed at the end of the day. One of those emerging was a pretty woman about Solomon's age with long hair, a sweet face and a quick step. Solomon moved from the wall and fell in next to her, walking a bit faster than his usual pace to keep up, although the woman was wearing three-inch heels. They had walked side by side for several steps when the woman began talking, still walking and not looking at her companion but as if talking to herself.

"For my next boyfriend I want an accountant. They are such smooth talkers, and I love to hear that accounting jargon. Makes me all aquiver."

Solomon in like fashion continued walking and looking straight ahead as he answered.

"Herman is sorry for everything and wants you back."

"In his bed. Under the sheets, not under the chupa."

"Yes under the chupa. A wedding, a good, old fashioned Jewish wedding. But it is hard for him to propose if you won't even see him."

At that Deborah Goldman stopped, turned and looked hard at Solomon. "You sure you want to get in the middle of this?"

"I am in the middle. Deb, he gives me such tsoris every day about you."

Deborah reached out, took his arm in a tender gesture. Her voice was softer. "You want to come for dinner, then we can talk afterward? I've got a lot of stuff in my head, maybe I'll ask your wise opinion."

"My opinion is you should marry the boy. But if you want to invite me to eat at your house, your mother being the best cook in at least the entire world, in trade for listening to your…stuff, sure."

"I'll bet you tell all the girls their mothers are the best cooks."

"Please don't tell my mother, will you? I get sick of my bachelor cooking and go home coupla times a week, so I wouldn't want to insult Mom, but the truth is your mother could out-cook my mother with one spatula tied behind her back." "I'm riding the bus. You driving?"

Solomon smiled, gestured. "Parked two blocks over. Should you call to warn her?"

"No, this just means there will be fewer leftovers. She always cooks a little extra, just in case. A little extra, just in case…how many times have I heard her say that? You know, I'm not learning her recipes. Got to do that, got to learn at least some of her magic."

"Herman will be counting on it."

"So if this accounting thing doesn't work out you could be a matchmaker already."

***

A few hours later Deborah, Solomon, and Deborah's parents, Irv and Simka Goldman, sat at the dining room table, all a bit glassy-eyed from the dinner they had just shared. Simka reached out, pushed the large platter that had been filled with brisket when they started, now nearly empty, towards the family's guest. "Look, Solomon, one small piece meat, it shouldn't go to waste."

Solomon could not make an emphatic gesture, but only wave a hand weakly. "No, I can't, Mrs. Goldman, thank you. Save it for a lunch for Deb. Or for me if she doesn't want it. But I am …" He stopped, patted his belly gently "I told Deb that you may be The Best Cook. Period. The Best. Mr. Goldman, I think it is amazing you don't weigh three hundred pounds."

Simka waved him off with a dismissive smile, then stood to start clearing the dishes, and Deborah immediately joined her. Solomon started to rise but both women quickly gestured he should stay. "Sit, talk!" said Simka. "This takes a minute."

Solomon sat back, turned to look at Irv Goldman, a short, solidly built man with large arms, his hands folded under his belly. "The secret, Solomon, is the box and barrel business keeps me moving, lots of lifting. When I was a kid I had arms like sticks. Now... so I eat, and I lift and I eat some more. Max and me own the place, but both of us are in the warehouse, on the loading dock, all the time. Max has arms like these too."

"You were skinny? Sorry, no offense meant...."

"No offense. Yes, skinny like a broom straw. You get married, you go into the box and barrel business, one day you look like you never looked before. So, how goes the accounting business?"

"Good, good thank you. I started with people I knew from high school and college, all Jewish, but now I am getting some who aren't Jewish, they like my work. In fact, another few clients and I will need a bookkeeper, an assistant. And that will mean a larger office, so it's a big step. I'm holding off, but in the next year I think so."

"Mazel Tov."

At that moment mother and daughter emerged from the kitchen, Deborah carrying a plate of cookies and some small dishes, Simka an enormous Jell-O mold. Solomon groaned. "Please, not your chocolate chip cookies. This is torture."

Simka Goldman nodded in sympathetic understanding. "Maybe just one, and some Jell-O. It doesn't take up any room, just runs down into the cracks."

***

Twenty minutes later Irv Goldman went to the front porch to smoke a cigar, and Solomon and Deborah went into the back yard to stand and look up at the Milky Way, bright over Toledo. After admiring the stars, the great smear of light across the sky, they walked to and sat in the aluminum and web-strapping lawn chairs. Solomon sighed. "It's a particular kind of pain, this overstuffed business. I mean, I did it myself, right? No one working that fork but me."

Deborah nodded, also under the spell of the brisket and potatoes and green beans and salad and tea and coffee and Jell-O and astonishing cookies. "You learn how to take small portions and to insist on no more. That you can do. Leaving food on your plate you never can do." Deborah stretched, settled more into her chair. "But enough about you and your digestion... You want to talk about my ex-boyfriend? Talk."

"This is ridiculous. He loves you like he could die, he has a good job, he wants to marry you... so you'll get married, you'll have children, I'll do your taxes. What?"

They sat a while under the summer night sky, in the small, dark back yard, just a little light from windows in the neighborhood, countless stars clear above. Solomon waited, sinking into a soft, comfortable state. A nap in the back yard maybe? Then Deborah spoke softly. "I almost did something so stupid I would have regretted it for the rest of my life. Regretted... and could not be fixed. Couldn't be made up for." Again she paused. "My mother lives for me and my father. We are her life, we two. All she wants is they should live forever then die on the same day, but not before I have many beautiful babies for her to feed and spoil."

Deborah turned, leaned toward Solomon. "But first, The Wedding! She has been planning my wedding from the moment the midwife said 'It's a girl.' So what do I do? It's not enough that I have sex with my almost-fiancée, and if the rubber breaks it's the end of the world, no, I almost talked him into doing it without a rubber. I wasn't drunk or angry, just a moment of stupid, he hesitates, and it doesn't happen. So I leave, and I'll bet he thinks I'm mad at him."

"You aren't?"

"No, that 'under the sheets' junk I gave you was just that, junk. But the problem is..."

"Oh, please...I am so confused."

"The problem is we have been dating for a year, and having this crazy stupid risky sex for six months, and we have to stop or get married. If I got pregnant and had to elope it would kill Mom, and down the aisle with a six-months belly wouldn't work so well either. I can't break her heart like that."

"What am I missing? So start again, humor me, I'm an accountant, not a social worker..."

"That friend of yours doesn't want to get married yet. Someday he wants to marry, and I know it's me he wants... I can't be mad at him, that is who he is. He is Mr. Herman Moskaivitch, a Man Not Ready To Marry. Look, Mom and I never talk about it, but she thinks, or at least hopes, that I'm a virgin. She never asks about where Herman and I go, sometimes I say a movie, over to some friends house... this is not a good thing, lying to one's mother, especially when all she does is adore me. And she hasn't asked about the breakup, just a brief comment about hoping things will work out. She never asks, never pries. And I lie to her and risk that wedding she's always dreamed of." Deborah began to cry softly, tears on her cheeks under the summer sky. "I'm a shmuhk. A shmuhk without a shmuhk." She wiped her face, reached into her skirt pocket, extracted a small pack of tissues, blew her nose. "And did you see her restraint with you? She's wondering what's going on... have I taken up with Herman's best friend? Are you here to help me win him back? Are you here to plead his case? To use her expression, she is biting her tongue until it bleeds. My mother." She shook her head in wonder.

Solomon opened his mouth, started to say something, but gave up, uncertain what advice to give. Deborah continued. "So OK. So now I say to him that I can't do this anymore, can't take the chance, I just can't. Two choices, two bad choices...... he walks away, and takes my heart along in his pocket. Did I tell you I love him? I love him. Lots and bunches. Don't want him to walk away. Choice number two, he marries me, but not because he wants to, but because I force him, I force him with guilt and sex and he resents and someday we divorce and you and the lawyers split the pie. So, Nu? Which is worse?"

"How about I don't give you a snappy answer? I need to think. But I will say this, a request actually... In the meantime don't fall in love with anyone else, will you? Give him a chance..."

"Solly, I'm not going anywhere." She put her hands flat down on her thighs, brightened, ready to change the subject. "And how's by you?"

"You think you're the only one with secrets? Have I got a secret for you! Your future husband knows but no one else. Our secret, right?"

"My sad story, our secret, right?"

"Done."

"Me too."

"OK, Deb, try this one on......do you believe in love at first sight?"

"Both my parents swear that is what happened to them. Sure, why not? Who knows what chemistry this love business is. Or maybe the religions that teach we go round and round have it right..... maybe they were married a thousand years ago. Who knows? So, you love her at first sight or she loves you?"

"I was at Wickstein's to do the books, they had a funeral for that young man, Darren Manion, you see that in the paper, killed in a motorcycle accident?"

"Yeah, I think I remember him from high school. Terrible."

"Deb, there is no easy way to say this. I'm in love with his widow."

"What do you mean, what…"

"I got in the receiving line, I shook her hand, I looked at her face, I fell in love. Is that the stupidest thing you ever heard?"

"Falling in love is never stupid. What the love makes you do….now that can be really stupid, let me tell you. So….. what? Now what?"

"Well, I went to the house three times, took wine and candy for the family, but just talked to them, family, visitors, you know, shiva-sitting conversation. I just said goodbye to Molly as I was leaving, I swear it. No hustling."

"Molly."

"Molly. Widow Molly Manion, new widow Molly Manion, and I'm in love with her. Thanks for not laughing out loud."

Deborah got up out of her chair, came to his, stood close to him, bent over and kissed him on top of his head, then gently patted where she had kissed. He looked up. Her eyes were bright with almost-tears in the soft light, a sweet smile on her face. "You are a serious, careful accountant, Solomon Wohlman. If you say you're in love then I have no doubt it's true. The question is what are you going to do with this one-way love of yours."

He reached for her hand, squeezed it. "I'm going to wait until I think the time is right and ask her… for a….. a date? Hell, I don't know, Deb. I don't know."

"Remember when we could hardly wait to grow up?"

CHAPTER SEVEN

I n Clearwater, Florida, a wife and mother of three children walked up the front steps of her home, a bag of groceries in each arm. Just as she reached the porch her heel caught on a the head of a nail. Although sticking up just half an inch it was enough to cause her to stumble, and she tried to save herself and the groceries as she fell on her side.

Herman had just gotten home from work when the phone rang.

"Hello?"

"Herman, I need to talk to you. Something has happened."

He answered with deep concern. "Deb, what's wrong, what's happened?"

"No, sorry, didn't mean to scare you, nothing bad, well, sort of... I just need to see you. Can you meet me at Inky's in an hour?"

"Deb, what's going on? You don't talk to me for three weeks, suddenly something's up and let's share a pizza?"

"I know, it's... please, Herman."

Inky's was far and away the favorite pizza joint, teenagers and young adults and families with young children, Italians and Jews and Blacks, students from Central Catholic and Scott and DeVilbiss High Schools and the University. A typical pizza place; booths, wooden tables, Formica, no tablecloths, people dressed casually.

When Herman got there Deborah was already seated in a booth, silverware and water glasses for two. He slid in the opposite side. "Hi, Deb. What's up?"

"Honey, I ordered already, mushrooms and black olives. And grape pop."

"Did I hear honey? Was that for me?"

"Yes it was. I'll even give you another. Honey, my cousin Janice, the one in Florida, broke her arm. Tripped on the top step of their porch and fell, I guess it's pretty bad. She and Fred are going to need help with the kids for the next month or two, maybe more. I'm going to go. Two reasons. To help her, and to think about us."

Herman started to say something but Deborah made a waiting gesture with her hands. "Let me finish. Oh good, here's the pizza. You eat, I'll talk."

A waitress brought a pizza, two large glasses filled with ice and two bottles of grape pop, two straws and two plates to the table. Herman took a piece and started to eat. He said around the pizza "OK, I'm eating, you talk. Please."

"I want you to have time to think about us. Take the time while I'm gone, and I will too. For now, here's what I think." Deborah folded her hands in front of her. "There is a line, a ready-to-marry line. I stepped over that line, some time ago actually. You haven't. I think you've got your toes right up to it, but you haven't stepped over. And that's all right…I'm not wrong to be where I am, and you aren't wrong either, on your side of the line."

"I'm sorry."

"For what? For not being ready to marry? I might as well apologize for being ready."

"On the other side of the line."

"Yes. Neither one of us wrong. Just that darn line."

"What about your job? And aren't you going to eat some pizza?"

Deborah picked up a piece, took a small bite, set the slice on her plate. "I'll explain the situation to them, got a family member in a desperate situation, and if they want me back that'll be fine... they probably will, they like me. But I can't say now exactly when I'll be back, so if there's nothing available when I do... well, I do good work. I can find something. Not worried, they'll give me a great reference, I know it." She took another bite of the pizza. Herman was starting on his second slice. She looked at him with a serious, straight-forward expression. "Remember the last time we were together?"

"Could I ever forget?"

"I said let's go for it, and you hesitated. You were right. I am so glad you hesitated. So glad." She suddenly slid out of the booth and stood. "Stay, enjoy the pizza. Here, here's money, my treat, and my address in Florida. Write me, no phone calls, letters, OK? We'll both take the time to write letters." She moved fast, was quickly gone.

***

As Deborah had expected, her employers said they understood the emergency, that they thought she was a wonderful employee and they would try to re-hire her when she returned, if not at least give her a splendid reference. She packed and left for Florida. Herman missed her. Solomon concentrated on his work. Another two weeks passed.

***

Late in the afternoon Solomon sat working, as usual surrounded by files and file folders and work in progress, things so busy that he had a box with files sitting on both his guest chairs, the one by the wall and the one in front of the desk. There was a knock on the door, and without looking up Solomon called out "Come in, Herman." He heard the door open and looked up. Standing there was Molly Manion.

"Mr. Wohlman? I'm sorry to drop in without an appointment... May I speak with you a moment?" She remained in the doorway. For a tiny moment Solomon was frozen, then he jumped up and almost tripped going around his desk, taking the box out of the chair and setting it on the floor, straightening his tie, all the while saying "Please come in, Mrs. Manion, sorry, let me move that box. Please have a seat."

Molly Manion was dressed in a dark suit, a small hat with tiny veil over her forehead. She had a file folder in her hands. As she sat Solomon stepped quickly to the wall and took his suit coat off the hook, slipped it on, tugged on his tie again and returned to his seat.

"I just left the bank downstairs. Mr. Wohlman...my husband Darren, may he rest in peace, had a six thousand dollar insurance policy with double indemnity. One of the bank officers is a friend of my father's and I visited him for advice. He wrote out a list of my options, gave me some papers......but I'm lost...buy bonds, get an annuity, invest in real estate...I've got enough to buy a house, pay cash! But I don't know for sure if I'm staying in Toledo, permanently, that is, but for now I am....so many choices...as I was walking out I glanced at the office directory and saw your name, saw you're here, right here on the second floor of the bank building. I thought...could you please look at all this and make some sense of it for me? Just tell me in plain English what the two or three best choices are."

"Certainly, I'd be pleased to." He reached in a drawer and got out a clean file, wrote Mrs. D. Manion on the edge, then reached for a pen and pad. It felt good to be on familiar ground. She handed him the folder, he set it down without looking at the contents.

"Please, I need to ask you some questions to help me suggest those best choices."

"Of course. What do you need to know?"

"Do you own your home or rent?"

Molly smiled a small smile, his heart ached, his face stayed professional. "I can make this easy on you. We were just starting out. Rented apartment, a four-year old Packard, paid for, about a hundred fifty in savings... that's all."

"And do you actually have the funds yet...the insurance settlement?"

"Yes, it came yesterday. I couldn't do the paperwork at first, just too hard. Then when I did, I don't know why it took this long to come, almost a month... but... I put it in the bank. Downstairs." She opened her purse, took out a small bankbook with a dark blue cover and tiny gold lettering. "Before today it said one hundred fifty dollars and seventeen cents. Now it says twelve thousand one hundred fifty dollars and seventeen cents. It doesn't even look real." She shook her head slightly, put the book back in her purse and closed it with a soft snap, then stood and he did too. She offered her hand and they shook briefly. "Thank you so much. My phone number's in the file...please call when you're ready."

"I can bring it to you."

"Thank you, no, I'm spending too many hours in the apartment...there or his parent's house. It helps to get out, to have something to do. I'm a school secretary, school starts in three weeks and I'm ready to go back, to be busy. I'm thinking of taking some college courses, too, so please don't invest all my money."

"Next time I'll have a place for you to sit."

Molly glanced around the office. "You're very busy. That must mean people trust you with their money. I will too." She started moving towards the door, and he stepped quickly around her to open it for her.

"Goodbye, Mr. Wohlman, and thank you."

"I'm pleased to be of service. Goodbye, Mrs. Manion."

She walked out and he waited a moment then closed the door carefully so it wouldn't slam. He stood another long moment looking at the closed door then suddenly dope-slapped his forehead. "I'm pleased to be of service" he muttered, a pained look on his face. "What a way with words. What a cement-head. What a schmuck."

***

Ten days later, Solomon sat in his office, trying not to keep looking at his watch. He had spent part of the last several days cleaning and dusting his office, finally giving in and buying another filing cabinet, so now there were almost no files out. He had looked and looked for something to brighten up the office, and finally settled on a small picture of daisies and carnations in a white vase on a peach tablecloth. And he had found cushions that exactly fit the wooden guest chairs, both of which had been carefully wiped with a cloth, then some lemon-scented furniture oil, then again with a dry cloth. The battered desk and desk chair had been treated with a light stain that hid many of their flaws, then desk and chair received their own wiping with lemon oil. He had his coat on, a crisp white shirt, the tie carefully tied, and it was a new one, bought at the Lion store, with a high silk content, costing double the dollar sixty he usually paid for ties. When he heard the knock on the door, he pressed his palms together, urged calmness upon himself, and called out "One moment, please" as he rose from his chair and moved to open the door.

He opened the door for Molly Manion. "Please come in, have a seat. I'll get your file."

As Solomon moved to his newest filing cabinet and slowly, with just a bit of ceremony, extracted her file, Molly did a quick survey of the room, her eyes scanning the painting, the clean desk, the organized office. She sat, and as he turned to walk to his desk she reached down and briefly touched the seat cushion, then folded her hands on the purse she held in her lap.

Solomon opened her file, turned it so it was facing her, and moved it towards her edge of the desk. "I don't know what your understanding of investments is, so let me start with some basic information. If I get too...elementary, please tell me."

Molly looked up from the papers, nodded, looked back down.

"There are very risky investments that have the chance of paying off big, but also failing completely. Obviously I would not recommend those. Nor would I recommend putting all your money in the most conservative investments, because you should give yourself a reasonable, safe chance to grow with the country, to hitch a ride on some of the better opportunities. As you said, twelve thousand is enough to buy a house, a comfortable house in a good neighborhood, with money left over. But doing that would take away your flexibility. And since you don't know if you want to stay in Toledo, or when you might get married again..." There was the tiniest of pauses. Molly did not look up. "...I think you have two choices, both good."

Molly pointed at the pages open in front of her. "Option A and Option B."

"Yes. In option A you buy a house with a large down payment. This means that you can easily pay the mortgage, taxes and insurance out of your salary and still have a comfortable amount left over. The balance of the money is in treasury bonds, tax-free municipals and some blue chip stocks that have performed well over many years, companies that look like they will keep going in that direction. This is a good option if two things are true..."

Molly raised her eyes and looked directly at him.

"First, if you think it highly likely you will stay here for at least five years. I wouldn't advise you to purchase... to be buying and selling a house in less time than that. Not that you would necessarily lose, you might win, but it's best if your plan is to stay in the house at least that long. The second…truth… is whether or not you want the trouble of a house. It is a good investment, no doubt, and if you keep it ten or fifteen years, pay it off in that time, which you could, well, you would have a home free and clear, and that's a fine thing. But it means clogged drains, cutting the grass, repairing the roof, shoveling snow, water heaters bursting at three in the morning…"

"Or stay where I am and call the landlord at three in the morning."

"That's right. My best advice is to buy, buy carefully, take your time… But if you aren't sure about staying here, or you just don't want to worry about managing a house alone, then…"

Molly Manion, the widow with the deep dark eyes, said "Then there is option B."

"Yes, B… which is staying in your apartment, or some other place you rent, and investing almost all of it in a spread of tax-free and taxable bonds, government securities, and blue chip stocks….good, safe, steady growth with the potential for some really good news if the economy performs well. I've given you modest but reasonable projections of both plans, your home growing in value, your investments growing in value, five and ten years out."

Molly read the pages, looking back and forth between the options. He sat back in his chair, carefully allowing himself a glance at her downcast eyes, her nose, her lips. How much he wanted to kiss her. His face showed none of this yearning, he was all and only business.

Molly looked up, gave him a warm smile. "Thank you. This is exactly what I wanted. It's very clear."

"Mrs. Manion, would you permit me to escort you to Friday night services?"

They sat a moment, for Solomon the longest moment of his life. Then Molly spoke. "It's...been...nine...weeks..."

Solomon blushed, brokenhearted. "I'm sorry, I'm sorry, that was so stupid..."

"No it wasn't. I'm very lonely. I love going to Friday night services at Beth Shalom.... Yes, thank you. Yes. And maybe you should call me Molly."

"And maybe you should call me Solomon."

CHAPTER EIGHT

Thursday night.

M olly lay in bed, dressed in a long, cream-colored nightgown. The apartment was dark except for a nightlight in the bathroom and a small lamp with a sixty-watt bulb on a nightstand next to the bed. The nightstand also held a telephone and a picture of Darren, her favorite, a picture of him holding a double scoop chocolate ice cream cone and grinning like a little boy. She looked at the picture. "Darren, Darren my love, I have something to tell you. I'm going on a date. Imagine that, Darren, a date." She gazed at the picture a bit longer, then reached out and turned off the light, then rolled onto her back. "It's like this. Either I don't marry again, or I do marry again. I think it is yes, I do marry again. Which means there has to be a date. A first date. So this is my first date without you, Darren, my first date without you in a long, long time." She closed her eyes, her breathing slowing, sleep coming. "I miss you so much" she whispered into the dark, still room "I'm so lonely. Please understand."

Friday afternoon.

The day Solomon bought his used car he treated himself to a car wash, the complete kind where people get inside and squirt cleaner on the windows and wipe the dash and steering wheel and instruments. After that, except in deep winter, he cleaned the car in his parent's driveway, since he couldn't use a hose at his apartment complex. His parents were pleased to donate the water, it got them a visit from their son. Solomon enjoyed the work - the hosing and wiping and waxing and the results he produced - a change from the quiet of sitting behind a desk that was so much of his life, and he usually did some chores for his parents afterwards, working in the garden or washing their car, a good, sweaty, movement-filled few hours. But this was a special occasion, and besides he felt impatient, itchy, not in the mood for the slow process of cleaning the car himself. He closed his office early Friday afternoon, and took the car to a carwash on Detroit Avenue, near the intersection with Bancroft Street, a company that had been there as long as he could remember. He watched through the window while they washed and dried the car, paid the sixty-five cents plus a dime tip, then drove home, where he changed clothes and then went out and worked on the Chevrolet a bit more, polishing the windows and making sure there was no dust visible on any surface. Next he went inside and did some more polishing, this time his serious black wingtip shoes. He ate a brief dinner, leftovers from his last visit to his parent's house, then shaved for the second time that day, took a shower, washed his hair, brushed his teeth with exquisite care, used Listerine and then a mint-smelling mouthwash. He reached for the after-shave and realized he had only his usual, Old Spice and Aqua Velva, to choose from. He wished he still had some Canoe or Russian Leather from his last round of dating, but they seemed to have dried up along with the relationships. "Boring" he said to himself. Solomon then dressed in his freshly dry-cleaned suit, put on a new crisp white shirt, on sale for two seventy-five at Willard Clothing on Adams Street, and another new tie, dark and conservative like all the others. He took a moment to observe that he had a small collection of dark, conservative, boring ties. "You need help" he muttered.

Friday night.

Services started at seven-thirty. Solomon had promised he would pick her up at seven, and he pulled up in front of her apartment building at six-fifty. Actually he had left his apartment so early that he had driven slowly the entire way, cars passing him, and still had to sit a half block away for five minutes.

Solomon felt a strange combination of giddy excitement and absolute calm. Molly buzzed him into the building, he went to her door then knocked twice, not too hard, and she opened the door. This time she had on a dark blue suit with a silk blue blouse in a lighter, complimentary shade, and a thin gold necklace. Her only other jewelry were her engagement and wedding rings. They greeted, then he walked behind her to the car. He wanted to be a gentleman, to take her elbow, but didn't want to be too bold, maybe she wouldn't want his touch. So he walked close, opened the car door. They drove the short distance to the synagogue in silence, each with their heads so full of thoughts they couldn't decide what thing to say first, so they said nothing, the silence growing until it became impossible to break. Molly noticed how clean the car was, as she had noticed the cleaned office and the new cushion. When they arrived he parked, then got out and walked around to her side of the car. When he opened the door he offered his hand to help her and she took it, her gloved hand light in his.

People were arriving, single people, couples, families, older people helped by their adult children. Molly was known to many of them, Solomon to some, since his family belonged to B'nai Israel, and that's where he usually attended, but easily half of those attending knew Molly or Solomon or his parents or her deceased husband's parents, and those people looked and noticed and tried not to stare, although a few did, and a few of those already seated even pointed discretely behind their prayer books and made short, whispered comments. Molly noticed but had expected, anticipated the looks and whispers, so she said hello to some, introduced Solomon to others, and he took her lead, relaxed a bit and greeted friends and acquaintances. Soon the service started, and they both got into the rituals, the familiar songs, the comfort of the prayers in Hebrew and English, the worship based on beliefs from so long ago, the days of Abraham, Isaac, and Jacob. L'dor Va'dor, from generation to generation. During the sermon, their prayer books closed, Solomon's brain screamed at him to take her hand, but he resisted the urge, the desire.

The Oneg Shabbat was, as always, a calm, pleasant way to finish the week; first the service and then some time to chat with friends, sip tea or coffee, punch for the children, and eat from a display of a dozen or more styles of cookies. Solomon favored the almond cookies, a swirled design with a drop of chewy cherry candy in the center. Molly loved the tiny squares of lemon cake, only a bite or two each, a single piece of walnut on the top of each square. As they walked into the large room that was used for wedding receptions, bar and bat mitzvah receptions and Purim festivals and lessons in Israeli folk dancing and other occasions of Jewish sharing, people worked at not noticing, not staring. Solomon asked her if she would like coffee or tea and she said tea, so he poured a cup for her and one for him. They walked towards the trays of cookies and as they chose he was approached by one of his clients. Talking a bit of shop after services was not unknown. At that moment Molly saw one of her friends, a woman who had attended her wedding, now very pregnant with her first child. Molly walked to her.

"Hello, Susan. Looks like you're serious about this pregnant thing."

"Oy, Molly, I can't sit long, he presses on my bladder, I can stand only minutes until my swollen feet kvetch, forget about sleeping, all night long he's doing pushups and running track like his father did. He should wait until high school to do his sprints, it would be fine with me, but no, three in the morning his little legs are churning."

"I hear a lot of 'he,' Susan. You sure?"

"I think so, have from the start. My mother thinks so, the doctor thinks so. So of course it will be a girl."

"Of course. How soon?"

"Three weeks, twenty-one days exactly, that's the prediction. A little early is fine by me. Meanwhile Harvey has the room all ready, we don't know a boy a girl, so we found some light blue wallpaper with pink flowers, that should work for either sex for a few years. Did I just say sex? Nine minutes for the man, nine months for the woman. Such a deal! And for the first six months Harvey was still finishing his residency, so I never saw him. Which was good for him, he was spared three months of listening to me throw up. Oh, sorry, terrible thing to say as you try to eat lemon cake."

Molly laughed. "That won't stop me. Watch." she said, finishing off the small yellow square. "So how is the doctor?"

"He's fine, knock wood. Look at him over there with his head together with Toplosky and Miller. Three doctors. Wonder if it's medicine or golf they're talking about? Not that he got to golf much this year, but next summer he'll be out there."

"Best place to get suddenly sick is a hospital, next best is a shul."

"Yeah, and Miller's OB - GYN. I go into early labor he can deliver the baby right here."

Molly laughed again.

"So Molly, are we good enough friends for me to ask about the man you were sitting with?"

"Is there some way I could say no to that question?" As Susan looked a bit stricken Molly hurried to assure her. "I'm teasing, Susan, yes we are certainly good enough friends, and I'm glad to tell you. His name is Solomon Wohlman, he's an accountant, has his own shop. He came to the house when we were sitting shiva, knew someone in Darren's family, I think. Anyway, we didn't... I don't have an accountant, never needed one, but Darren, may he rest in peace, had an insurance policy and I didn't know what the best thing was to do with it. Not that it's a fortune, it isn't... who buys that kind of insurance? But it was enough that I wanted some good advice, so I asked him and he gave it, really good, clear advice."

"So then... wait, the feet just quit on me. Please, come sit a minute." They walked over to where padded folding chairs were lined up against one wall and sat, one chair between them so they could turn toward each other. "OK, so if this is not a good question, now you really could tell me to get lost."

"You want to know what giving me investment advice has to do with Friday night services."

"Yes, I should be so bold."

"He asked to take me, I said yes. There's really nothing else to say."

"I'm sorry, that was a tacky thing for me to ask."

"No it wasn't. Lots of other people here wondering, I see their eyes turning then turning away. Think it looks like a date to them? Looks like one to me."

"You know, we, some of the girls and me, we thought you'd move back home, Chicago, right?"

"Yes, I thought about it, but I don't want to go through packing and moving and looking for another job, and my mother would mother me to death, it just wouldn't work. I like being a school secretary, and I'm thinking maybe I'll go back to college, get a teaching degree. At least I'm going to go talk to them, see what it would take, how long."

"Good for you. You know if you ever need anything..."

"Thank you. Everyone has been so kind. It's really amazing."

"We look after our own."

"Yes we do, but the warmth, the love, it's not just yiddishkayt … it's also been others, Darren's co-workers, even though he was there such a short time, and my people from school. Lots of love from everyone."

Susan reached over, patted her hand. "Good…good." She paused. "Well, time to take the doctor home, I can spend a few minutes with him. You know what's good about being married to an orthopedist? They give great massages, know all those muscles and connecting parts."

"Those muscles and connecting parts can lead to more children, I've been told."

"Five, no more. Oy, listen to me, four more times I'm committing to!"

They hugged briefly then separated. As Molly walked toward Solomon he saw her coming and seemed to conclude his conversation, shaking hands with the man he was talking to and starting to walk towards her.

"You didn't have to stop for me, I'm in no hurry."

"No, thanks for rescuing me…. I'm happy he's a success already, enough with the celebration. I've heard the story twice before. Are you ready to leave?"

"Yes."

On the way home they talked briefly, mostly Molly talking about Susan and the impending birth, Solomon listening, driving oh so carefully. He walked her to her door, his brain screaming at him again, this time to take her in his arms and kiss her sweet mouth, but reason prevailed, and when she offered her hand for a shake and said "Thank you" he shook it and said "You're welcome" and then she was in her apartment and he was heading back to his car, happy and a little dizzy from how much he wanted to speak to her of love.

CHAPTER NINE

A week had gone by. For Molly it had been a busy week. School would start soon, and she had offered to come in early to make sure the school office was ready for the onslaught of students and to assist any teachers who wanted help ordering supplies, setting up displays, designing bulletin boards.

Her principal and several of the teachers had attended Darren's funeral and sat shiva with her. They had asked if she was returning to the school in the fall and she had said yes, probably yes, but no one would have been surprised if she had decided to move back to Chicago, so her principal was pleased to hear from her, pleased to know that she was returning. Back in the elementary school, getting ready for the return of the young children, the young – excited – exciting - so alive children, no one knew how to talk of death, so all her principal, her teacher friends said was "Please let me know if you need anything, any help." Molly smiled, thanked them for their kind offers, and continued working, pitching in, storing old files, helping an elderly teacher move books, organizing a new section of the library.

Molly didn't spend much time thinking about Solomon. The investment advice he had created, the neat portfolio he had given her, lay on top of her dresser. She had been leaning towards staying where she was while she sorted things out, staying in the apartment for a least another year; packing and moving were unnecessary chores if she was comfortable there, and she was. She didn't feel it was haunted by Darren, since he had died on Telegraph Road, not in the apartment. His memory could haunt her anywhere. So Molly had used part of Option B; about half of the insurance money was still in her savings account, the rest in certificates maturing in six months and in a year, offering slightly higher returns. Solomon had considered, for just a moment, not billing her for his services, but he sensed, knew, that would not be appropriate, so he billed her for his hours and she paid him promptly and no more was said about it.

So Solomon wasn't much on her mind, an occasional fleeting thought. Darren was much more on her mind. His love, his presence, his death, his absence would not be whirling in her head all the time, not always filling her thoughts, as when she attended a meeting on a modified attendance record-keeping system for the new year, or went through jars of paste and finger paint, helping the kindergarten teacher decide what had to be ordered. But now and then, again and often, he would pop up, or rather his not being there would pop to the front of her consciousness. "Oh, Darren" her mind would say, sometimes unexpectedly. Of course coming home to the empty apartment was never easy, cooking and eating alone was never easy, getting into the empty bed alone was hard, heartaching.

Solomon waited a week to call, gently to approach her, carefully to build a relationship.

"Hello?"

"Hello, Molly, it's Solomon."

"Solomon, hello, how are you?"

"Fine. How is the school year starting?"

"Busy, busy. It feels good, actually. We've had students for two days, the kids are all wide-eyed and excited. Lots of paperwork, new families, that sort of thing, but a good beginning. And you, your work?"

"Going fine. I'm going to need help this coming tax season, I know that. I might see if I can find someone part-time, maybe a housewife who knows bookkeeping, someone who'd like to work at home. I think I'm going to run a want ad in the next few weeks."

"A growing business."

"Yes, a growing business. Do you like going to the art museum"

"...ahh... you changed the subject, didn't you? Sure, sure I like it."

"Would you like to go next Sunday, just walk around and visit some favorites?"

She said yes before she thought about it, just said yes. They agreed on his picking her up at one o'clock. After hanging up she stopped and thought about what this meant, that this was, no doubt about it, a date. Going to Friday night services might be considered more the sharing of a religious experience than a date, but this was a real one, and she had so many emotions and feelings about it that she chose not to deal with the swirl of them, but just to go, see the paintings, enjoy.

***

Thursday Solomon ate at his parent's house. Dinner was fine, the brisket good, although a bit dry. Solomon had given a report on his business, had shared some community news with his mother and father, caught up on family news and was quietly slicing his boiled potatoes when his mother said "So I understand last week you went to Friday night services."

"It's nice to know the Jewish grapevine is alive and well, although a little slow. I mean, it was a week ago."

"A widow you took?"

Solomon put down his fork, leaned back in his chair. "Now, dear mother, I think you know exactly who I took. In fact, you no doubt know where we sat and how many cookies we had with our tea."

"Don't be silly. I only just heard you took Molly Manion, so recently a widow, what a shame."

"Yes, what a shame."

Solomon resumed eating. He turned his face just slightly towards his father, and they exchanged winks. The quiet at the table continued, the questions forming in the air like gathering clouds.

"So I was wondering….."

"Sylvia, leave the boy alone. He's all grown up, he's earning a living, he wants to take widows to shul or even dancing that's his business."

"Denzing!" Sylvia said, her left hand to her heart.

"Thanks, Dad, that helped a lot" said Solomon with a smile. "Mom, she's a client, I'm helping her with some decisions she has to make. She's Jewish, her family is in Chicago, she's lonely. I took her to services, we said the prayers, we kibitzed with friends, I took her home."

"Sort of a mitzvah" his father said in his defense.

"Yeah, a small mitzvah, that's all."

His mother nodded. "Yes, I understand. Of course, it helps to do mitzvahs for widows if they are young and also I understand very pretty."

"Yes, she is young and pretty. She is also a client, and slightly, a little bit, a friend. Now let me guess, the next thing we're going to talk about is how happy my brother is being married, and how happy you both are to be married….."

"Your brother is happy, but if they should have children already he would be even happier."

Marvin rolled his eyes and returned to his dinner.

"One more question, if you don't mind. You going to take her to shul again?"

"Yeah, I think so. She's nice to talk to. So Dad, you think the Tiger's pitching can hold up? Newhouser should be good for another strong year."

Baseball took over for a short time, leaving the woman of the house out of the conversation. When she was able to rejoin it they talked about some of the programs at the Jewish Community Center on Collingwood, and Solomon told them he was going to be part of a panel in November on personal taxes and investing. This took the discussion to money, business, news of the day. The pending date at the art museum wasn't revealed, and widows and happy marriages were not mentioned again.

***

The Toledo Museum of Art is a treasure for the community and the entire country. Founded soon after 1900, the museum was given a tremendous head start by donations from the Libbey family, the Libbey fortune made from the development of glass production methods and products. Rembrandt, Matisse, Van Gogh, modern art, Egyptian art and artifacts, sculpture fill its hallways and galleries, separated by large round pillars of cool marble. For those who like to personally connect to history there are small bottles and jars, some of them five thousand years old, that held potions, lotions, makeup. Women wearing makeup can stand and gaze at a bottle that held makeup five thousand years earlier.

The museum has been a location for polite, genteel dates since its inception. It is a safe place to be, an expression of intellectual concepts, and a way to explore common interests, should they exist. Does he like the Egyptian artifacts? Does she share his fascination with modern art? Do they both admire the magic of pointillism, those paintings that change as you walk towards and away from them?

Solomon picked Molly up right on time, the car again spotless. He spent a long time worrying over his clothes and finally settled on a button-down shirt with a sweater, no tie, wool slacks and freshly shined penny loafers purchased while he was in the Army that were still in good shape. Molly wore a dress. Dresses made up much of her wardrobe. As a school secretary she felt obligated to wear a dress, or a good quality skirt and blouse, every day, since her principal and most of the teachers, almost all female, dressed in similar fashion, the few men wearing short or long sleeved shirts but always with a tie.

As on most Sunday afternoons the museum had many visitors, and, as usual in the summer months, many from out of town. People wandered from one collection to another. Solomon hadn't planned what they would see, where they would go, and so they just started walking, looking. Nothing special or momentous happened, not that Solomon expected it to. They just looked, and commented, and shared, and then he took her home. How much he enjoyed being with her. How much he wanted to be with her more, all the time, every day.

***

A pleasant date, a visit to the art museum, the chance to wander and compare notes and interests, the chance for Solomon to steal a peek at her eyes, her dark eyes and eyelashes and smooth neck and quickly glance away and look at a painting so she doesn't catch him, doesn't see him admiring her when he should be admiring the work of an artist from hundreds of years past. A pleasant date. Now what?

The answer came in the form of a flyer from the Jewish Center. It was a notice of the upcoming Jewish Book Fair, an event Solomon had paid only scant attention to in the past. But now it seemed to be the perfect answer, exquisite timing.

Like the museum it was a chance to have something to look at and think about and compare notes and interests, a focus of their mutual attention, their focus elsewhere, not on each other. He did realize that he would have to be very calm, no stealing of peeks, because members of the community, people who know them both, would be everywhere. He would just be the calm, unemotional accountant, escorting his widow client, no masher he. He also believed people would instantly suspect what a fraud he was, that he was really in love with her, as if he wore a sign around his neck: "Never mind what I say, I'm head over heels for Molly."

The book fare was two weeks away, so this wasn't really rushing things, three dates in about six weeks. Still, when Molly accepted the invitation she did so with a feeling of uncertainty, almost unreality. She just couldn't get used to the idea that she was unattached. It kept feeling like something was wrong, missing, and of course something was; her husband, the love of her life. But she was going out on a date, and that was all right, because she wasn't married. So strange. So upsetting. And yet she didn't want to sit home alone, and this nice Jewish boy wanted to take her to services and the museum and a book fair; gentle, civil pursuits. Intellectual pursuits. Pursuit of her.

Solomon of course offered to pick her up again, but this time, keeping a bit of distance while she continued to sort through her emotions, she asked if she could meet him there. So on a bright Sunday afternoon he stood, browsing, watching the door, having gotten there twenty minutes before the agreed-on meeting time of one o'clock.

Molly was punctual, entering the Jewish Center at two minutes before one. He saw her and smiled, walked up to her and they shook hands. She had told him that she had never attended a Jewish Book Fair before and was looking forward to the experience. They started by browsing, much as they had at the museum, part of the time side by side.

Many of the books were about the events of the past ten years: World War II, the Holocaust, the establishment of Israel, the Balfour Declaration, Theodor Herzl, Chaim Weizmann. There were cookbooks, collections of stories, books about the Torah and worship practices, the history of the Jewish people, about growing up Jewish in America. Other books: Eddie Cantor and his role in the development of the Screen Actors Guild, a book about the life and work of Ernest Bloch, another about the influx of brilliant Jewish scholars and scientists from Germany and Eastern Europe between the early 1930s to 1941, two about Alfred Einstein. At two o'clock an author spoke about his book, a collection of recipes and folk stories from Russia, Poland, Lithuania, and Austria.

Soon after that they left. It was a warm and pleasant afternoon, so she left her car at the Center while they drove north a bit, near the Michigan line, and stopped at a small stand that sold fresh cantaloupe served in quarters with a large scoop of vanilla ice cream. Delicious. He drove her back to her car, aching that the afternoon together was ending so soon.

CHAPTER TEN

S o you remember Deborah went to help her cousin in Florida, leaving Herman so they could both think about marriage. Here's what happened.

Deborah took the bus to Florida, two long days from Toledo, but she found she could nap part of the time and look out the window at the changing scenery as they rolled past fields of various animals, plants, shades and colors. In the winter you could take Greyhounds from Toledo, the Sun Bow in 32 hours, or the Sun King in 31 hours, through service to Florida, on-board restrooms, even steward service, although rather expensive; $21.75 to Saint Petersburg and $24.00 to Miami. The summer trips cost less but took longer, lots and lots of local stops. Deborah knew that it would take four or five days for letters to move between Clearwater and Toledo, so she decided to get the letter writing campaign started early. She found she could write on the bus, although she had anticipated it would make her nauseated, as reading in a moving car always did. But perhaps it was the height of the bus or that she could scrunch down, turn her back to the near window and write in relative comfort. She had purchased stationery, a light cinnamon color, envelopes to match, plenty of three-cent stamps. Her plan was to have a letter ready to mail somewhere along the route, some rest stop, or at worst when she arrived in Florida.

Herman: We just left the stop in downtown Columbus, heading south. Well of course heading south. Guess I've decided to write everything, even my stupid stuff.

The bus is nearly full. I'm sharing my seat with a sweet old lady, going to visit her brother in Clearwater. She got on the bus in Detroit, what a long ride. She said he is trying to convince her to move there, give up the Michigan winters. Anyway, I have a nice companion all the way there.

I'm looking forward to getting lots of wonderful letters full of wit and wisdom.

I love you.

Deborah was surprised to see that she had ended the letter so abruptly, but, well, there seemed nothing more to say at this point. So she addressed the envelope, put a stamp on it, licked and sealed the envelope and put it in her purse with her other writing equipment. She mailed it at the next rest stop.

The two women chatted from time to time, and Deborah listened to stories of the elderly woman's family through a gentle haze, knowing that she could forget the information even as she heard it. The woman didn't like the bright sun coming through the window, so she requested the aisle seat all the way to Florida, which pleased Deborah. The ride was long, tiring, but afforded her some good sightseeing as the bus moved through Kentucky and Tennessee and rolled past the red clay fields of Georgia.

Her cousin's husband, Fred Kander, who she hadn't seen in more than a year, was waiting for her when the bus arrived. They hugged, then he grabbed her luggage, two suitcases and a small box.

"The box, as you probably guessed, is full of food. Mom is convinced that you can't get Jewish food once you go south of the Ohio river."

"So what's in it? Can't be fresh corned beef."

"Bottles of borscht, wrapped in layers of newspaper, some pickles she put up, kosher dills, and I think a jar of her pickled green tomatoes."

"I can taste them already. That was sweet of her. But actually the supply is decent, picking up. We've had so many New York and New Jersey retirees moving here, and they insist on their delicacies, so things are getting better in the deli department."

"So how's my cousin?"

"The arm gives her a twinge now and then, but it was a clean break, the doctor said it will heal fine, just take some time to get her muscles back, to get her arm strong again. He said that when she is sixty she'll be able to predict rain with it, but aside from that it there shouldn't be any problems."

Fred helped Deborah with her luggage. The sun was, to Deborah's skin, burning hot, a heat lamp. She realized that she had erred in packing only short-sleeve blouses, that she needed long sleeves and a straw hat. They drove the ten miles to the house with all the windows down, the hot air whipping through the car. By the time they arrived Deborah was already feeling thirsty and lightheaded, her skin scratchy. As she emerged from the car the front door opened and the two little girls, Niomi and Raya, came flying out of the door and down the steps and front walk. Deborah squatted down.

"Hello, my sweet nieces. Do you remember me?"

The children slowly, sadly shook their heads no. "But I remember your face because Mommy showed us your picture we have a picture book it's full of pictures and I saw you in it" said Niomi.

Deborah laughed and said "That's good, but now you get to see the real thing. We'll be such good friends."

"Can you take us to the beach?"

"Kids, kids, relax, let your aunt rest a minute" said Fred. They started up the walk, the children circling, dancing, when the door opened again and Janice stepped out onto the porch. Her right arm was bent at the elbow and held by a cast that went from her wrist to just below her shoulder, all held by a sling made from a gigantic red and black and white farmer's bandana. Her other arm was clutched around the baby boy, Asher.

"Hey, Deb, welcome to Florida."

"Hey, Jan, you know, I would have come just to see you and your family, including that latest addition on your hip. You didn't have to break an arm to get me here."

Deborah continued up the walk, started up the stairs and paused, looking at the porch.

"All taken care of" said Fred behind her. I sunk it deep with a nail set, filled the hole with plastic wood, sanded it, ended up sanding and painting the whole porch."

"He loves to fix things around here" said Janice, leaning forward so Deborah could hug her. "You hungry? Thirsty? Bathroom?"

"Bathroom, thanks, then liquid. My goodness it is hot in Clearwater in the summer, isn't it?"

"Yes, a bit warm today. You'll get used to it. What I don't understand is getting used to Ohio winters. I mean, five below? What kind of number is that?"

"Can I ease your burden? Will he let me hold him?"

"The ultimate friendly baby," Janice said, giving Asher over to Deborah. "His sisters have him convinced he's a live doll, so he goes to anyone without a fuss." Deborah went inside and the family followed. A while later they were sitting at a round table, a beach umbrella over them, the sun starting to descend in the late afternoon. A pitcher of lemonade was rapidly disappearing.

"I can't believe you're really here, Deb. This is so darn hard, I mean, I didn't want to complain when you first considered it, didn't want to twist your... no, I don't want to say that. But I'll tell you, now that you're here I sure am glad." She reached out a hand, squeezed her husband's hand. "Fred is great, so helpful, what a lovey, and the kids try, but they're so little...."

"Yeah, I can guess it must be hard cooking, cleaning..."

"Everything. We don't own a clothes dryer, hang up the clothes on the lines, they dry in minutes. But hanging clothes is not a job for someone with a broken arm. Yes, and cooking.... and, between us girls, personal things are hard to do. So you are more welcome than I can ever say, and I don't know how we'll ever repay you."

"I'm just piling up serious mitzvah points, never can tell when they might come in handy. So is there anything you need done right away?"

"Enjoy your lemonade....."

"Jan, I've been sitting for the past two days. I need to move some, it'll feel good. Great. Don't worry, I'll rest, in fact I'll sleep like a baby. Sleeping on a bus is... well, it's more like passing out, you get so tired that you just go away for a while, but it sure isn't eight hours solid... I think four was the longest stretch."

"Want a nap now?"

"Put me to work!"

Janice laughed. "OK, Deb, take the kids down to the beach."

"That's not work."

"I need some peace and quiet. I need some time to talk to my husband without 'mommy mommy mommy' going on. And I might take a nap, that sounds luscious."

"Can I borrow a hat? And something with sleeves? I brought the wrong things, no hat, all these Ohio soak-up-the-sun clothes."

The beach was only three blocks away, and the children tugged at Deborah to walk faster, pulling like energetic puppies. They had a glorious hour and a half, running a few feet into the surf, having the waves chase them and splash over them, Deborah holding the baby tightly while the waves splashed his feet as he squealed and bubbled his delight. Then they washed off the salt under a public shower head set on a slab of concrete and headed home. When Deborah got there she realized she was starved and exhausted. They were greeted by the smell of hot dogs and hamburgers on the grill Fred had going in the back yard. A splendid meal.

Naomi gave up her bed, doubling up with Raya, a guarantee of wrestling matches and giggling for many nights to come. Deborah curled into the small bed and instantly fell asleep.

The next day, right after breakfast, they all got in the car and headed downtown for the shops on Myrtle Avenue. First priority was a straw hat for Deborah. That found, they visited several shops where she bought some light cotton long-sleeve blouses, and prepared to become a true Florida lady.

As soon as she got back to the house she took out her writing equipment, went onto the porch and began to write.

Herman Honey Bun: Well I sure didn't understand about this sun they have down here, I don't think it is the same one we have in Ohio. Almost got burned bad the first day, they rescued me just in time. Went shopping, picked up a big straw hat and some blouses that cover my arms but I still have to be so careful.

Jan is doing fine, in good spirits and her arm aches only some, once in a while, but taking care of the children sure is hard. They have her in this big cast that gets in the way, so it isn't just the loss of the arm but this clunky thing all the time between her and what she's trying to do.

Fred leaves tomorrow, he's been around and doing chores so not much to do, but there will be lots and lots to do starting tomorrow. He has to leave, will be on a business trip for a couple of days, so here I go right into the deep end... which reminds me, they have an ocean here. Did you know that? I could say this is a lovely place for a honeymoon, but I won't.

I miss you. Aren't you glad you've already written me twice?

Deb

When Herman got the first note he felt a little pressure, but nothing like the feeling that descended on him when he got the second, since he hadn't even bought stationary, let alone written a word or thought about what he might say. Now he had to rush something to Deborah, which meant not three cents but air mail, six cents.... no, this called for special delivery, thirteen. Well, a dime punishment for delay, that sounded appropriate. So he quickly wrote the letter, the next day rushed to the post office on his lunch hour and paid the price.

After waiting for several days, half hoping though not really expecting that Herman had written to her within minutes of her bus departing, Deborah was surprised when the postman came to the door with a special delivery letter for her. All eyes on her, she opened it and read.

Deb: Sorry to have taken so long to write back, I'll really try hard to do better next time. Work is fine, kind of boring, I know all the routes and drivers and can run the operation without really thinking about it, so that's not good, right? I mean, I should be doing more with my brain. Maybe a new job, you can give me some advice when you get back.

Things are kind of quiet. I go to the deli or Inky's with Sol.

Say hello to everyone. I miss you.

Herm

Deborah didn't expect great letters from Herman, nor loving ones, at least not initially, but even so the first one was disappointing. The way it was delivered heightened the excitement of getting it and thus the letdown of its unromantic nature. She felt he was saved by the last three words. "OK, let's keep this going" she thought.

Sweets: I love giving advice. Maybe sales? Sell trucks or machinery or cars or something manly like that. You're a fun guy and people like you and I'll bet you could sell like crazy. We will talk.

I'm now a full-time helper, Fred is gone on his short business trip, I'm doing laundry and dishes and helping with the kids, watching over them. They sure take a lot of energy. Not complaining, though. Is it all right if I say I like kids, or is that being tricky pushy?

Keep those cards and letters coming.

Deb

Their letters crossed, his arriving just two days later. It contained a surprise.

Deb: Stopped over to see your parents. They're fine, your mother can still cook like nobody else, but it wasn't the same without you there. Well, in a way you were. Your mother got out your baby pictures again. What a cute tush! I think those pictures of you with your clothes off made me crazy, because your father beat me good, took eighteen cents from me. Distracted by a tush, not the first man to have that happen. Your mother couldn't stand it, after I was there over an hour she finally asks me if I think we'll get started again when you return. Of course I said yes, and she was so happy she gave me a second dessert.

I miss you more.

Herm

Deborah read the letter over twice. I miss you more, it said. I miss you more. More than what? More than he use to? More than she misses him? More than her parents? Was that just an incomplete sentence or a very clever device? And he had visited her parents! OK, these are positive signs. Suddenly Deborah missed him terribly, loved him so deeply.

Two days later, Fred had returned and was taking the children for a late afternoon romp on the beach. Deborah and Janice declined to go, and instead spent a short time doing chores and making preparations for supper, then retired to the porch, the air hot but the shade, and slight breeze, delightful at that hour.

They sat, relaxing, sipping iced tea with a touch of sugar and lemon.

"Janice, feel like offering some love advice, some…ahh, pre-marriage counseling?"

"Haven't I been a well behaved cousin, not asking you what was in the letter? Been wanting to ask…."

"When you were getting close to marriage, did either one of you get cold feet?"

"Both of us. But I think that happens to most folks, don't you? Lifetime decision, who goes into that saying I have no doubts?"

"Oh, my… well I feel that way. I don't have any doubts…..but maybe that means there's something wrong with me. Not really grown up or something."

"No, I didn't mean it that way. It isn't proof of maturity to be scared. So you're all ready, huh? That's good. So what kind of advice you want? Herman's feet not as warm as yours?"

"I don't think there's any question about us getting married. I mean, he loves me. We get along great....but he can't seem to make the final decision, to propose.... I mean, I'm not going to propose, that's a good old fashioned thing that I want him to do. The man proposes. Right?"

"Right!"

"How did Fred propose?"

"Oh this is so corny. We had a dumb fight about something, I don't even remember what. I go to the movies with a bunch of the girls, he calls and my mother says I'm out on a date. He goes nuts, I get home he's there, starts yelling at me all about aren't we going steady and what am I doing out on a date with another guy just because we had a little fight. So I tell him that I was with my girlfriends, not on a date, and what is he so mad about anyway? Then he shouts at me, shouts, I'll never forget, 'because I love you and want you to marry me.' Face all red, what a picture. So I say to him 'Did you just propose?' That was it. Well, not exactly. Some hot kissing, I think we would have done it right there on the living room floor if my mother hadn't been in the kitchen."

"Did you ever ask your mother about saying that you were on a date when you really weren't?"

"She just gave me the old shoulder shrug, you know, what's the difference between a date or going with my friends. Sure, sure. I think Fred got flummoxed by my mom."

"Seems to have turned out all right."

"Well, she got the grandchildren she wanted. I'm kidding... yes, it did turn out all right. Splendidly so. I married a prince of a guy, handy around the house, helps with the kids, very romantic at times. I'll be glad to give advice, but I think it's like the best way to live long is pick the right parents.... the best way to be in a loving marriage is to marry someone loving."

"Got one of those. He's so good....he's the one. My Herman. Deborah Moskaivitch, not exactly musical but it sounds just right to me."

"And the needed advice is....."

"I'm ready, he isn't, we're both feeling..... feeling...wrong. I'm wrong pushy he's wrong timid. Like that."

"How long you been dating... serious dating?"

"A year, bit more."

"Can you be cool a bit longer?"

"I think I have to be. Yeah, not another choice, is there?"

"How are the letters going?"

Deborah poured some more tea for both of them. She took a long drink, leaned back in her chair, rolled her head several times. "Fine, I guess. Neutral letters, you know, signed 'love' and nice words... I can't seem to behave myself. Sent him a note telling him I thought this might be a nice place for a honeymoon. Shame on me."

Janice smiled. "How'd he react?"

"Nothing yet. But he did send a note saying he missed me more."

"More than what?"

"Exactly my question."

"Ain't love grand?"

They smiled at each other. Deborah got up, went into the kitchen to do some pre-dinner preparations and to have a moment to herself. When she returned to the porch she stood there and looked down at Janice. "That's it, Jan, isn't it? My choice is one choice, wait."

"Unless you... oh, do I want to say this?"

"You do. Please."

"Unless you think he's never going to be ready to settle down."

74

"I've thought about that, but, no, I just think he's not ready, ready now. You know, he didn't finish college. His best friend, Solomon Wohlman, finished college, in fact he's a CPA. Herman's got a kind of dead-end job…pays OK, but I don't know what the chances of moving up are. So his career, what he's going to do next, it bothers him. It's a fairly big company, headquarters in Atlanta, so he's just another guy to them. And he feels like he's not using his brain, he's said as much before and just said it again in his letter. So that's bothering him too."

"But those things, his education, the job, they don't slow you down, do they?"

"No, I just think things will work out. He's a hard worker, a nice guy… I think that an opportunity will turn up. And I like working, I can work for a while, have some kids, then when they're older I can go back to work.… the thing is, I don't see any of it being a reason for waiting."

"I'm what, six, seven years older than you? Bit reluctant to sound too worldly wise, but my advice is to relax a little, see what happens when you get back."

Deborah took a few steps, bent down and hugged her cousin. "I know you're right." She stood. "I also know the chicken isn't going to cook itself, or the onions jump in the pan for browning without some help."

"Browning onions. What a wonderful smell. I'll come, sit in the kitchen and we'll keep kibitzing. You cut the onions, I can stir left handed."

***

Weeks went by, letters back and forth, now and then.

***

There came a day when the mailman walked up to the house in Clearwater, opening the mailbox on the fencepost next to the front gate. It had been four days since the last note from Herman, and Deborah had hopes of getting one that day, or in the next two or three. She opened the mailbox and took out a small pack of bills and letters and a copy of LIFE. There was a letter from Herman. Deborah took the items into the house, put the family mail on the kitchen table in front of Janice, who was drinking coffee, and sat down in a kitchen chair. Janice glanced at her, then picked up the magazine and started flipping through the pictures, being carefully uninquisitive.

The envelope yielded a hard, plain white card, with nothing on it. Blank. Deborah turned it over and saw a line drawn across the middle from one side to the other, cutting the card in half. Below the line there was nothing. Above the line were hand-drawn pictures of two pairs of shoes, one pair men's shoes, one pair women's shoes, in the style of shoes used to diagram dance steps. The shoes were close, facing each other, toe-to-toe. Above the shoes was written PLEASE! Deborah stared a moment, got it, and shouted with joy. She jumped up, spun and danced around the room. "What, what?" said Janice. Deborah stopped, handed the card to Janice who looked at it and then back at Deborah.

"Might you stop dancing just a moment to tell me what this means?"

"It means you and Fred are going to have to shlep the children all the way to Toledo. I mean, you wouldn't miss my wedding, would you?"

A few weeks later.

Deborah was home again, had been home three days, to her parent's great joy. The first two days she had been unpacking, calling her former employer to discuss returning, running errands, helping her mother. Now things were settling down. The evening of the third day she sat quietly eating, nestled in love, her mother urging her to have another generous helping of salad, the green food was so good for her. Deborah sighed contentedly. "I missed this so much. You, dad, the comforts of home…"

Irv Goldman nodded approvingly. "You did a mitzvah, a real mitzvah. So many weeks you gave them." Simka Goldman also nodded approvingly, beaming. "Your aunt Rachel called me again this afternoon, telling me how much you did for them, she can't thank you enough for helping Janice and the family…here, have some more potatoes."

"One! A small one, please." As her mother put a potato on her plate, Deborah turned toward her father, giving her mother an opportunity to spoon a second potato her way. Deborah sat looking at her father, a serious expression on her face. "Dad, Herman is coming over later. He wants to ask you something."

Both parents froze in mid-eating, raised their eyes to each other. Then Irv turned to his daughter.

"He wants to ask me something?"

At this Deborah allowed a tiny, mischievous smile to begin.

"Yeah, he wants to ask you something."

Simka Goldman whooped, clapped her hands.

"Come help me in the kitchen a minute, Deborah. Come on." The two women almost sprang from the table and hurried to the kitchen. A moment later brief shouts and short bursts of laughter were heard, while the man of the house shook his head and continued eating. Shortly the sounds stopped, and Deborah and her mother returned, very calm, as if nothing had happened. Simka spoke to her husband. "So, nu, you want dessert now or when the boy comes?"

"I don't know. When he comes, when he goes…let me see what happens with this question and answer business, then I'll tell you."

The family returned to their routine. Irv smoked a cigar outside while the women cleaned up. Even outside he could hear the occasional laughter. He came in, picked up the newspaper and sat in his usual chair. A typical evening in the Goldman household. The women fussed with the house, fussed with their appearances. He ignored them as best he could.

The doorbell rang.

Deborah spoke up, brightly, like a school girl. "Now who could that be?"

Irv remained seated, buried in his paper. Simka didn't know what to do with herself, so she hovered in the arched opening between the dining room and kitchen. Deborah went to the door and opened it. Herman was standing there, wearing a tie and sport coat, his hair carefully combed. He looked flushed and nervous. He stepped inside, Deborah closed the door, Irv lowered his paper enough to see their visitor, and everyone waited.

The man of the house took control. "Hello, Herman. Been a while. How are you, how's the family?"

He answered in a rush. "Fine, sir, we're all fine. And hello Mrs. Goldman. And Deborah."

The women both answered him, almost as one. "Hello Herman." The tableau held, Deborah standing near, Irv in his chair ready to lift the paper and resume reading, Simka standing in the kitchen doorway quietly squeezing the life out of the dishcloth in her hands. Then Herman took a deep breath and said "Mr. Goldman, I wonder if I could talk to you alone for a moment." He turned, his eyes taking in first Deborah and then her mother. He spoke so respectfully. "I'm sorry, if you would please excuse us."

Simka said "Certainly. Deborah, you make some tea while I get dessert ready?"

"Sure, Mom."

Deborah almost skipped to her mother's side, and they hurried into the kitchen, whispering.

Irving Goldman looked towards the kitchen, then back at the young man standing near him. "Nu?"

Herman stood there, the very picture of uncertainty, then moved to a nearby chair where he perched uncomfortably on the front edge of the cushion. "Mr. Goldman....."

At that, the older man gave Herman an exaggerated, conspiratorial wink and with his large, muscular hands indicated that he should wait a moment. Then he stood, moved to the couch, sat down and signaled for Herman to come sit next to him. Herman stood, walked to the couch, and sat where indicated. Irving leaned forward, spoke in a half whisper. "Shaa, softly, it will make them crazy. So let me guess. You want to marry my daughter. I also want you should marry my daughter, so stop sweating already. And loosen that knot, I can't breathe when I look on you."

Herman smiled a smile of great relief and did as instructed, taking an enormous breath and letting it out dramatically. Irv Goldman nodded his approval, saying "Much better. Much better, now we both breathe more easy." He pointed towards the kitchen.

"Let's sit here a little longer, make them even crazier. So I'm asking you, you want to come in the business?"

"Mr. Goldman..."

"Irving. Call me Irving. Or Irv. Look, you don't have to decide right now, but...I don't have a son to leave my half the business to, and Deborah isn't going to wrestle with barrels and trucks all day, so...maybe you want to come in the business. You should excuse me saying this, but Deborah once told us you aren't so crazy about that job of yours. So maybe it would be good for you, and it should make me happy if you say yes. So like I said, let me know. Either way you decide I welcome you, blessings on you both. Welcome to the family."

Sitting on the couch the two men shook hands firmly. Once more Irv leaned in, again with the whisper. "Now, maybe you don't know about me and my bride, but a little bit we are practical jokers. All our years together, a little trick we play now and then. Nothing mean, but a good joke is better than diamonds. So now you and me, we going to practical joke those women. I'm going to shout something angry at you. You shout the same words angry right back at me. The same words, good and angry. OK?"

Herman looked a bit dubious. "OK."

"Don't be so afraid, just a joke, you'll love how we do them."

Herman squared his shoulders, gave a brave smile. "I'm ready, Irv. Let's practical joke those women."

All this time Deborah and Simka Goldman stood in the kitchen. They had taken a few moments to prepare the desert, boil the water for tea and fill the best teapot, saved for special occasions, but they had soon run out of things to do and now fidgeted, waiting, trying to hear something from the quiet front room, meeting each other's eyes and shrugging.

Irving Goldman, conspiracy leader, stood up and walked carefully to the front door. Herman stood too, but stayed close to the couch. Irv opened the front door as quietly as possible, turned towards Herman, gave one more broad, conspiratorial wink, and suddenly shouted, loud and angrily, "To hell with you!" To which Herman loudly responded "Yeah, well to hell with you!" At that Irv Goldman slammed the door hard.

In the kitchen the women exchanged looks of astonishment and horror, stricken with disaster. They moved through the doorway and the dining room, unconsciously each holding her hands clasped tight together. As they turned the corner towards the front room they saw Irv Goldman standing, pointing, his face clearly

SOLOMON THE ACCOUNTANT

saying "Gotcha!" Herman stood with his hands in front of him, palms up, helpless surrender.

Simka reacted first. "Irving Goldman! You could cause a heart attack with your foolishness!"

"Yes, my dear. Is dessert ready?"

Simka folded her arms. "There is no dessert for nobody in this house until somebody says what's up."

"What's up is the children are getting married and maybe he comes in the business should he want to. Is the tea getting cold?"

That was it, the damn broke. Deborah hugged Herman, kissed Herman, hugged and kissed her father, Simka hugged Herman and kissed his cheeks and gave them a pinch. "Such a scare you gave me. You should not let that crazy husband of mine teach you such bad manners."

"I'm sorry...."

"For nothing. It was a good joke. Now I need to find one to do him. So you want some tea and cookies?"

***

Later that evening, after tea and cookies and raspberry Jell-O, Herman said goodbye to Irv and Simka. Deborah walked with him to his car, and they stood next to it, reluctant to end the evening.

"So how do you feel, now that you've taken the big step? Scared? Regretful? Rethinking it already?"

"Honestly?"

"No other way."

"Now that I've taken the big step... by the way, I will never forget your face, you and your mother's faces, when you came into the living room."

"I know it was Dad's idea, otherwise you would be in such trouble. But you're ducking the question. Regrets?"

"Enough already. No, dear, no regrets. In fact, I wish it were tomorrow. I wish we were getting married tomorrow."

81

"It'll take a bit longer."

"Like how much is a bit longer?"

"Well, finding an open date at the shul, and then all the caterers and flowers and photographers and invitations and other mishegoss ...six months. About six, seven months."

"During which time we do it or don't do it?"

"Don't. Sorry, but I came too close to the edge before. I'm going to do this right... for my mother.... for me."

"Which counting the time you've been laying around Florida means no sex for almost a year! This is not so wonderful."

"But I'm worth waiting for."

"But you... are worth waiting for."

"And...you're not the only one waiting, mister! If you remember, you weren't bouncing around that bed alone. I miss it too. But I promise you this, you better take two weeks vacation for our honeymoon, because..." she stepped very close to him "...you'll be spending that second week in the hospital..." then she raised her hand and poked him in the chest with every word. "... Getting. Testosterone. Replenishment. Therapy!" Deborah kissed him quickly and jumped back. "So get your rest, future husband, you'll need it."

"Do it and do it till our wheels fall off."

"So very charming. Goodnight. By the way, I love you." With that she turned and ran back to the house.

***

Not far from where Canton and Cherry Streets meet was the G&P Bag, Barrel and Drum Company. This was the oldest Jewish neighborhood in Toledo, settled before 1900. Originally largely residential, with butcher shops and small stores and a few synagogues, it had become, by the mid-1950s, an area of fewer homes but more small factories, not far from heavier industrial sites, including large yards where rusting cars were stripped of everything useful and then crushed into cubes for shipment to the steel mills of Detroit, Cleveland, Steubenville and Pittsburgh.

G&P wasn't a factory, but a warehouse, a place where large trucks brought in paper bags by the thousands, mashed flat and bound with wire strapping, barrels of fiber with metal rims at the top and bottom, smaller drums of fiber and wood. All day large shipments arrived at one end of the large cement-block building, were unloaded and stored on racks by type of item, later to be disbursed to businesses in northwest Ohio. Customers would come and purchase a dozen or a hundred bags, or ten barrels, or six drums. Larger customers would have their purchases delivered, and some of the relationships went back many years.

Herman had decided to take his father-in-law up on the offer to come into the business. Why not? He was already working in the trucking business, understood dispatching, so it seemed like a logical next step. Plus he could probably end up making a decent living. Plus it would make Deborah happy, always a good thing. He took a day off work to visit G&P. He hadn't given his employer notice, but he was pretty sure he wanted to make this move, just wanted to talk to Irv Goldman and his partner, see if there were any signs of danger, that he might be making a mistake, although he really didn't expect any. He hoped today went well and that he could give his two weeks notice the next day.

The parking lot was made up of limestone from quarries near Lime City, just south of Toledo, white rocks that over time, from the weight of truck after truck, became almost a pavement of white stones all stuck together. Every few years, as dirt worked its way to the surface, another ten tons of large-piece limestone was dumped and smoothed over the more heavily used portions.

Herman drove his 1947 Studebaker two-door Commander Regal Deluxe into the parking lot and parked away from the building, near the fence separating the company from its neighbor, a store selling batteries and battery cables for trucks and cars and industrial uses, Al's Battery and Wiring. He walked across the crunching white driveway and into the front door. As he did so Irving Goldman, sitting at a cluttered desk, looked up and spotted him. "Herman, welcome. Come, let me give you a tour."

"Thanks, Mister Gol... Irv."

"So you know from truck dispatching, right?"

"Sure, that's what I do all day."

"So that part of the business you'll understand." Irv got up from behind his desk and they walked from the small front office area into the large open area that made up most of the building. "As you can see, a tiny office space, me and Max and the bookkeeper and our inventory maven, that's what we call Irma, our inventory maven, she does dispatching and takes care of the inventory, works with Claire our bookkeeper. You know, you come in the business I think the first thing you do is look for new customers. Me and Max, couple of alter kockers, we serve the same people for a long time. Sometimes a new one, he walks in the door, he heard about us somewhere, but the city is growing, and other places, some of the small towns we never visited, we could have more business, still we could handle it here. So maybe you would do some business calls, sales calls?"

"Sure, I'd like that."

"So what you think?"

"My goodness, I'm overwhelmed. You're offering me the chance to join a healthy company....."

"Not just join. Own. Someday my half belongs to you and Deborah and, should you be blessed, your children."

"This would be a dream come true for me. I don't know what to say."

"Come, you should say hello to my other half.. my business other half." They walked into the storage and distribution area that was more than three quarters of the entire building, an open section with the roof supported by steel beam pillars. Racks and dividers separated flat cartons, fiber barrels and paper bags, a variety of sizes, mostly brown or beige, a few of the bags white. NO SMOKING signs were attached to each pillar. At the far end the truck bay doors were open, large trucks unloading, small trucks and a few cars loading, people signing receipts or bills of lading. In the middle stood a small, solidly built man with close-cropped, almost all gray hair. He looked up from an inventory list and saw them coming, walked over and stuck out a hand, large and strong like his partner's.

"Herman, good to see you again, been a long time. Welcome, Mazel Tov. Such good news I'm hearing."

"Thank you, Mister Perlman."

"Nah, call me Max, you're going to come into the business, right?"

"I guess so. I mean, yes, this is overwhelming, to be offered a chance to join, some day own half of a business."

"Maybe not half the business..."

"I'm sorry, Mr. Perlman, I didn't mean..."

"No, no, remember, Max, call me Max….No, you should own at least a half, who knows, maybe all the business. This pisher Irv thinks about himself, about bringing in a son-in-law, keeping it going. You know what he wants? He wants it in good hands. This makes sense; we, Irv and me, we don't want to let the business die, and who knows if we could find a buyer, especially a buyer at a fair price. So you come, you work, you learn, one of these days he could retire and you keep it going. This is as it should be." At this Max Perlman took a step and put an arm around Herman. "But Herman, I'm even older than this old man" he said, nodding towards Irving. "Tell the truth, I could think about retirement right now. We've got a daughter, married, two children, a teacher. In Arizona. Arizona! We've been there four times now... beautiful land, beautiful. We want go visit, spend time, maybe live there. Maybe my wife and I grow old in Arizona."

"That could be very nice" Herman said.

"Nice, yes. But! I also have a son, a doctor, he's now a resident in a Jewish hospital in New York. He might end up anywhere... but you know, me, my wife, we've never been to New York. So we want to sell our piece of this place, cash out, visit New York, visit Florida, lots of time in Arizona, maybe someday even see Las Vegas, Los Angeles... So I sell you and what's-his-name my part for a fair price and everybody is a happy person."

Irving waved a dismissive hand at his partner. "Go, retire already, I'll send you a nickel once in a while. And a pickle. A nickel und a pickle."

"You see, Herman? You see what I put up with all these years? All these years..."

"You must be very proud of your children."

"May you and Deborah be so favored one day. Let me tell you... my father, of blessed memory, was a tailor. One day he has to run for his life because the Russians are murdering the Jews. He comes to America. His son, me, sells bags and barrels. His grandson, who he never got to see, is a doctor in a Jewish hospital in New York City. A doctor in a Jewish hospital in America, grandson of a man who ran with just his sewing needles from the crazies. Is this a great country or what?"

"Yes it is. America is a good place to be Jewish."

Max Perlman nodded his head, slipped his arm off of Herman and, facing him, gave him a firm handshake. "We sell you this place, me now and some day my partner, you take good care of it? You take good care of the workers, the employees?"

"Yes sir, I promise."

Irving spoke up. "So, when can you start?"

At that Max looked around, took it all in, shook his head as if weighted down by the burden. "So much to learn, so much to learn……"

"I have to tell my boss… Two weeks? Two weeks from Monday?"

Irving nodded in approval. "That is fine. Two weeks from Monday."

Max folded his large arms across his chest. "One more thing!" he announced.

"Yes?" said Herman.

"I love Deborah like mine own daughter. You take care of her, too. Understand?"

Irving leapt to Herman's defense. "What are you hollering on the boy for, Max? He loves her like he can't see straight. So when is your son the doctor getting married?"

"Right now he is too busy to… Herman, welcome to the family. Too bad about your father-in-law."

CHAPTER ELEVEN

B ut meanwhile, what about Solomon and his pursuit of Molly? So, I'll tell you. So, their fourth date. The first was to Friday Night services, the second the museum, the third the Jewish Book Fair. This time going to see Jose Ferrer in Cyrano de Bergerac at the Pantheon, downtown. Solomon had been thinking about buying a newer car before the winter, and he had made the purchase just the last week, moving up four years to a 1946 Chevrolet Stylemaster four-door sedan. A nice car in which to take a lady to a downtown movie.

After the movie they went to Franklin's Ice Cream. He had a dish of pistachio, she strawberry swirl. They sat in a booth.

"How is the school year starting?" he asked.

"This is my third fall, and it's the same as the last two, so I guess it must always be like this.... crazy. Families transferring in, records to get from other schools, medical, inoculation records, requests to change teachers..."

"Why requests to change teachers now? The students have barely met them."

"It's the parents... they want their Amanda to have the same third grade teacher older brother Randolph did, don't want the new teacher. Or the opposite, older child didn't like a teacher, had behavior problems, and they're afraid the teacher will take it out on the younger children."

"What do you do?"

"Well, the principal has to deal with it, glad I don't have to, but we say no almost every time. Just too much of a mess if we start saying yes. We'd have musical chairs for the whole first month."

"I see."

"Can I change the subject, Solomon? I'm curious about something. Actually, two somethings."

He smiled at her. "Sure, what?"

"Why did you come to the house that first time? When we were sitting shiva... who do you know in the families?"

Solomon paused. "What if I tell you the truth?"

"Do you know how to lie?"

"I don't think so, not without stammering and blushing."

She smiled. "So it sounds like you should tell the truth."

"Do you remember... this isn't easy."

"Now I'm really intrigued. Sol, pull the bandage. Tell me."

"Do you remember seeing me at the funeral?"

"No, but I wasn't...tuned in... not much at all. Mostly I was led around."

"I was there to do the books, some accounting, tax problem. When I heard it was someone my age I thought... it just seemed I should honor him... it just seemed wrong to start doing accounting work and ignore the families. Actually, I slightly knew someone...not important. I went there to do tax work, but since I was there I first went to pay my respects because a young Jew was dead. I went through the receiving line, I saw you, I wanted to see you again. Going to a home where they are sitting shiva because you want to see the widow again... I'm real glad that I wasn't hit by a lightning bolt. So, now what?"

"Now what? Why, you think I'll be angry? No, I asked, you told, I'm.... I'm flattered. I'm sure I wasn't very attractive that day."

Solomon wanted to move away from this uncomfortable subject, so he didn't tell her he thought her beauty shown through the pain and the tears. He said nothing, his heart pounding a bit.

"But that leads to a second something... no, wait, that makes three."

Relieved, Solomon took a spoonful of ice cream, waved the empty spoon. "Three somethings, one down, two to go. Ask away."

"What if I hadn't knocked on your door that day?" Molly glanced down, took some ice cream from her dish, then looked up at him.

"I was going to wait. I don't know, nine, ten months. Or maybe six. I hadn't decided, but one day I was going to call."

"I see."

They both ate a moment, thoughts and emotions whirling. After a moment Molly put her spoon down, reached out and touched his hand a moment, then took it back. He waited, his pulse up yet another notch. "Third something. Solomon, this is our fourth date, and you haven't even touched my arm. I feel like I'm fragile as egg shells. So when you walk me to my door, don't you think we should kiss goodnight, even a little peck?"

Her smile was sweet, her eyes warm and welcoming. Solomon tried to stop himself but her words, her smile and eyes unlocked the door to his heart and it all came pouring out.

"I am in love with you. I want no one but you, and I don't know what to do with it. I'm afraid of scaring you, offending you... I could propose right now..."

"Don't."

"See? You see? I'm so scared of saying or doing the wrong thing... We've never talked about Darren. There, I said his name. We haven't talked about Darren, and maybe you want to..."

"You are the sweetest man. OK, how about a personal weather report. Or maybe emotional financial statement for my accountant. Sol, I don't know, I don't know what to say, don't really understand what I'm feeling...I miss Darren, may he rest in peace, there, I said his name too, miss him, probably will forever. But I have to keep going. I like being with you. I don't know what that means. Does it mean I like you and maybe you are the next man I will love, or is it just that I am lonely and heartsick and I'm... using you, or letting you be nice, I'm being selfish..."

"No, no you're not..."

"You're being sweet again, but really, you don't know. I don't know. I said I like being with you, that's the truth. And tomorrow's another day... and that's true too, but beyond that I don't know what's happening in my heart. And I don't want to make such a puzzle out of this, just let life go on, see what's around the next corner. What happens, happens. Oy, did I just sound like my mother!"

"Amazing, isn't it, we go to make a point to someone and our parent's voice comes out of our mouths. OK, so - so what I said isn't a problem?"

"No, Solomon Wohlman, nothing you said is a problem. Love is a big word, such a big word, I just can't say it now, can't feel it. Don't talk about loving me. Maybe someday."

They finished their desserts, he walked her to the car and opened the door for her. They rode home with their thoughts churning; something was in the air, something was different. Ole Buttermilk Sky played on the Motorola radio. He parked in front of her apartment, came around and opened the car door, and as always she took his hand to help her. They walked to her apartment door, and she unlocked the door then turned toward him. "Sol, let's not work too hard at this, or worry about it. I like being with you. If you want to, let's just... continue..."

Quickly she took a step toward him and placed her right hand on his arm, offered her lips for a small, tender kiss. She leaned back, looked at his face, read what his eyes said, then kissed him again, her lips still closed, but this kiss lasted a tiny bit longer. "Goodnight Sol" she said. Then she went inside and closed the door.

CHAPTER TWELVE

D eborah had gone to Florida, Herman had proposed, Deborah had returned, Herman was accepted into the family and the family business. In about the same time Solomon had given Molly financial advice, had taken her on four dates, had been kissed by Molly. Still neither Herman nor Deborah had met Molly, and had only the briefest of updates.

Together at Rosie's, hot bowls of matzo ball soup in front of them to counter an early fall drop in the temperature, one baseball-sized ball per soup, the three friends talked.

"OK, nudnik. I have consulted this matzo ball, prior to consuming it, regarding the truth of one alleged Molly individual." Herman said, waving his spoon grandly in the air then swooping it down, cutting a large bite off his matzo ball. "The ball, which I am about to happily inhale, and I think that you are either making this whole Molly thing up, which you're being an accountant-type person is so totally impossible, seeing as you lack almost any creativity...."

"Which by the way isn't a bad thing in an accountant" Deborah added.

"....or else you are ashamed of her, or ashamed of us. So name your poison."

"Wrong, wrong. You want to know the deal?"

"No, I asked you because I don't want to know the deal. *Of course* I, we, want to know. So if she really exists, and there's no embarrassment working here, why come we haven't met her?"

"Now remember, boys and girls, this is a recent widow. I am going very slowly. In fact, I've been thinking that it is time I introduced her to you."

"Solly, how many dates so far?" Deborah asked.

"Does shul count as a date?"

Herman turned towards Deborah. "You see? Evasion. There is no Molly."

Deborah leaned across the table, gently patted Solomon's hand. "He is without understanding, but I've decided he's my life's work. I mean, the situation can only improve, right? So when and where would you like us to meet her?"

Solomon lifted his hand and patted hers in return. "Thank you. How fortunate Herman is to have you. A clear example of why one says congratulations to the groom and best wishes to the bride. So, to answer the question, date one was Friday night services, eyebrows raised by all those who know Molly, or Darren, or their parents, or me, or my parents.. well, let's say lots of necks on swivels that night. Date two was the art museum..."

"Good choice" said Deborah.

"...date three was the Jewish Book Fair. That was just before you returned, Deb. I thought about asking Herman to meet us, but it seemed... I decided not to. No offense, Herm."

Herman shrugged, spooned some soup from his bowl.

Solomon continued. "And date four was last week, went to a movie, Cyrano de Bergerac. So it's time for her to meet my friends. Yes it is. Suggestions on where, what kind of.... um, venue?"

"Venue my friend says. No wonder the girls all swoon."

At that Deborah gave Herman a punch on his arm. "Herman, just order some more soup or something."

Herman rubbed his arm, pouted briefly, then signaled the waitress. He ordered a sandwich. "Your father is working me so hard."

Deborah smiled at Solomon. "Solly, if you're brave enough, I'll tell you the perfect fifth date, the date where she meets me and my intended. Actually I'll give you the second choice and the first. The second is the four of us go to a nice restaurant, white tablecloths, you know, Northwood Inn or someplace like that. But first choice is you make dinner for the four of us at your place. The truth is, you see, the way to a woman's heart is through her stomach. You want to dazzle her, get her furs and diamonds. You want her to fall in love with you, cook for her. So simple."

"But I never..." said Herman

She turned to him. "Sweetie, don't say it. Quit while you're ahead. Barely, but ahead."

"The problem" said Solomon "is my apartment is so... boring, like my ties, like my suits. And I can't cook anything special, some salad and potatoes, maybe a chicken breast, some ice cream afterwards - just not exciting food."

"Simply astonishing. You boys are so dense when it comes to women. Solly, think about it. You want a woman to love you. We women want projects, we fall in love with projects. Look, Herman is my sweetie pie, and soon we will be so happily married, but one of the reasons I love him is the work I see ahead. Herman the unfinished."

"I resemble that remark" said Herman.

"So you invite Molly to your apartment, she meets your friends, and she sees the work she has to do, how she has to help you decorate... she's already noticed your boring ties, no doubt, so she'll see how big a project you are, and she'll fall fast in love. And don't worry about dinner, the only error you could make is to cook better than she can."

"You really think I should do this."

"Absolutely."

Herman's sandwich arrived, then he added his approval to the Solomon cooking idea. "Yep, I think the lady is right. And we can chat and become good friends. And she will be pleased to know that, next to me, she got the best catch available."

Deborah turned to Herman, smiled ever so sweetly, then reached up and pinched his cheek. "Not yet, my love, but you will be when I'm done with you."

***

Solomon rehearsed. "Please come to my apartment for dinner, I'd like you to meet two of my dearest friends" sounded best to his ear as he spoke out loud while taking a shower, while shaving. He wasn't sure if he should say closest or dearest, but closest sounded like he had hundreds of friends strung out along a line from close to far distant, while dearest, a bit corny perhaps, seemed best to convey how he felt about Herman and Deborah. A week from Saturday. Soon, but not too pushy. He cleared the date with the other two then sat by the phone in his apartment, Wednesday night, and got ready to call Molly. One more rehearsal, then he dialed her number.

"Hello?"

"Hi Molly, its Solomon. How are you?"

"Fine, thanks. And you?"

"I'm fine, thanks - Please come to my apartment for dinner, I'd like you to meet two of my dearest friends."

"Well, sure, I'd like that…. when? And who are they?"

Solomon felt a sense of relief come over him even as he answered. She had quickly said yes, what had he been so worried about? "A week from Saturday, if that works for you….."

"Yes, what time?"

"Seven, I can pick you up."

SOLOMON THE ACCOUNTANT

"No, I'll drive, really, I don't mind, I don't drive all that much."

"You're sure?"

"Absolutely. So who am I meeting?"

"My friend from as far back as I can remember, Herman Moskaivitch, and his fiancée Deborah Goldman. Usually Deborah to her parents, that or Deb to her friends. I know you'll like them."

"I'm sure I will. OK, week from Saturday, seven, your apartment, I need an address."

Solomon gave her the address and brief directions, Toledo not being that difficult to navigate, especially since the Jewish community was mostly in the Old West End or in neighborhoods growing west off of Berdan or Monroe Street or in Old Orchard.

***

The week and a half until the Saturday dinner moved at different speeds for the four participants. For Simka and Deborah Goldman almost every day was a rush, Deborah working all day and then coming home to plans and invitation lists. Occasionally she took a long lunch, meeting with a caterer or to look at bridesmaid dresses. Although the wedding was still months away both mother and daughter wanted as much resolved, taken care of, as soon as possible. A fast week.

Things moved along quickly for Herman Moskaivitch, too, learning a business and making sales calls on behalf of that business, trying to memorize and not consult the folders and brochures he carried with him. Sometimes his customers knew his line of products better than he did, but they welcomed him, said how pleased they were to see a new face in the company, Irv and Max hadn't been by to visit in quite a while. He also worked at developing new clients, finding companies to visit from the business pages of phone books for Findlay and Fremont and Defiance and Bowling Green and Monroe, Michigan and the southern rim of Detroit, dropping in cold sometimes, just stopping in to talk about bags and barrels and fiber drums.

For Molly Manion life moved in the pattern that she was becoming accustomed to, busy during the day, busy at the school with phone calls and parents and teachers and students. Then going home, or sometimes shopping or visiting with her friends, spending time with Darren's family, or going to a late afternoon movie. Some letter writing but mostly phone calls, to or from her mother and sister. They worried about her, and she kept telling them she was all right, that she would see them at Thanksgiving.

For Solomon Wohlman the days crawled. Why had he said a week from Saturday? Why not this Saturday? Because he didn't want to press her - but he *did* want to press her, to press on her, to hold her, kiss her, have her fall in love with him. Oy. A long wait, slow days, do the books, call on the clients, talk on the phone, think about Molly. Try not to think about Molly. Think about Molly.

Sunday he called Deborah. "OK, Deb, you thought this was such a great idea. So good, I asked her to dinner. So now what?"

"What do you mean now what? Friday, which by the way is five whole days away, Friday afternoon you leave work a little early, you self-employed person you. Go to the market, buy what you need, and anything you might need for cleaning. Saturday you clean the apartment, then you clean you, then you make sure the bathroom is respectable for a lady, and then you get ready to cook. You picking her up?"

"No, she insisted on driving - probably wants to be able to escape my evil clutches."

"Exactly no one believes that. Actually, I think this is better. Have things ready to cook but wait until she arrives.

Light some nice candles, you know, nothing too strong, a nice light scent..."

"I don't know much about candles except Hanukah and Yahrzeit candles, but I'll find something appropriate."

"Go to Lamsons, they've got nice stuff."

"You were saying, I wait to cook until she arrives?"

"She gets to see you fussing in the kitchen - so homey, so haymish - and meanwhile we three can sip white wine. Don't forget to buy a good white wine, maybe two bottles."

"What time are you coming?"

"I'm guessing you want us there when she arrives."

"Yes."

"We'll be there by a quarter of... eight, right?"

"Seven! Seven!"

"Oh you are just too easy. Yes, dear, seven, like you've told both Herman and me almost every day since you called Molly. Quarter of seven, well behaved. You know, I'm really looking forward to meeting her."

"Thank you, Deb. I love you."

"And I love you too, but I'm taken. And you're crazy gone for a recent widow, most interesting behavior for a conservative accountant."

***

Solomon spent the next week really trying to focus on his work, be really grown up and not obsess about Saturday night. He only partly succeeded. He wrote out the list of cooking and cleaning ingredients, put it away and then took it out to double-check. Thursday night his mother insisted he come for dinner – "We haven't seen you in almost two weeks!" – and he went with some reluctance. No good reason for declining the invitation, but he didn't want to get into another discussion about Molly. But his mother asked only some gently probing questions which he answered with as little information as possible until his father rescued him with a discussion of who the Tigers should have batting leadoff, who cleanup.

***

Nancy Manion and Molly would keep in touch by phone, which pleased Molly, and she made a point of visiting Jack and Nancy at least twice a month. The death of Darren had been hard on Nancy, the terrible pain of losing a child just as he was entering the world of maturity, newly married, employed, someday soon a father. Both parents missed their son, missed the promise of the future grandchildren, and grieved for Molly, so young a widow.

Molly wore her engagement and wedding rings. She had never taken them off, never considered doing so. Jack didn't consider their significance, but Nancy did. It was now almost half a year since Darren was lost to them, and Nancy wanted to ask Molly about her future, although she was afraid that doing so might hurt their warm relationship. Still, the thoughts nagged, so this time when Molly came for dinner Nancy had planned, rehearsed, gentle words.

The conversation was pleasant, limited to the usual topics; Molly's work, Jack's work, some local and national politics. After dinner Jack poured apricot brandy for all three, then excused himself to go into the living room and watch their new Sylvania television with its crisp black-and-white picture and read the newspaper. Molly and Nancy set their brandy aside until they cleaned the table and did the dishes, then they sat at the kitchen table and sipped the sweet drink.

Nancy reached out a hand and patted Molly's, then held it a moment. "Sweetheart, I want to ask you something. No, I want to say something. You're too young to stay a widow. You should be starting over some day. Is it all right that I said that?"

"Yes, Nancy, it's all right. More than all right."

"Good, I hoped you'd not mind. I love you, don't want you to be alone, stay alone."

"Me either. Actually, I've had a few dates, to Friday night services, the Jewish book fair... but it's hard. It just feels strange, like I'm in one of those dreams where people are all mixed up, you know, not in their usual roles. Here I am going out on a date, but how can I go out on a date, I'm married, no, I'm not married - it just doesn't feel natural. Not yet. But I'm trying."

"Anyone special?"

"Not special, not boyfriend special, but there is one, a nice guy, Solomon Wohlman. He's an accountant, has his own office. You know him or his family?"

"No, no - where do they go?"

"B'nai Israel."

"So, this is good. You like him?"

"Yes. But I'm not rushing anything. I think I have to mourn at my own pace - speed - no timetable. When I'm ready I'll be ready, I guess."

"Have you thought about not wearing the rings anymore? Oh, that was too personal. I'm sorry, forgive me."

Molly shook her head a bit, smiled. "No, that's OK Nancy." She put her right hand on her left, gently twisted the rings back and forth a few times. "I'm thinking. I sort of decided that around a year from - maybe after the unveiling. Maybe I'll go to the service, we'll unveil the tombstone, then soon after. "

"I shouldn't have said that, I should have left...this is your business."

"What, I should be offended that you care about me? Nonsense." Molly leaned towards Nancy, and the two women hugged.

***

Could a calm, logical accountant be nervous? Yes he could, and was. The apartment was clean, the bathroom disinfected to hospital standards. Food was ready, or ready to prepare, white wine just removed from the Frigidaire to warm up slightly, glasses still in the Frig chilling - Deborah's suggestion - and the clock moved slowly, slowly. At twenty before the hour Herman and Deborah arrived. She took one look at Solomon and said "Sol, will you please relax. Relax! This will all go fine."

"Yeah, relax. I mean, the only thing you've got to worry about is me telling fart jokes."

Deborah turned to Herman and held up a warning finger. "That's zero funny. Zero. You behave or no more almost."

Herman blushed a bit, and said "Deborah, not in front of the boy."

Solomon looked from one to the other. "What? Almost what?"

Deborah laced her fingers together, put her shoulders back and spoke like a prim school teacher. "No one is taking any chances on any pregnancies. But there are some - other things - almost..."

Solomon waved both hands in the air. "Stop. I get it, I get it."

Deborah and Solomon went into the small galley kitchen, and talked about the food and preparations, reviewing what had been reviewed several times during the week. The doorbell rang.

Solomon took a deep breath, got a pat on the back from Deborah, and walked to the door, buzzing the outer door to unlock then moved quickly to the stairs and down. There was Molly.

"Hi, you found it all right."

"Small town, Toledo. Easy to get around in" she said, walking up the stairs. He met her at the landing, and didn't know whether to go first or let her pass. He decided to walk just ahead and to the side. He showed her his apartment door, and then stepped aside so she could enter first, he right behind her.

"Molly Manion, let me introduce my two dear friends, Herman Moskaivitch and Deborah Goldman."

Molly and Deborah shook hands, then Molly and Herman. Deborah sensed an awkward pause coming and just smashed right through it. "Sol, get out that wine and those hors d'oeuvres. Herman, you see if you can help him." Turning to Molly she said "The reason I'm giving orders, although only engaged, is that I'm practicing for the real thing. You don't mind?"

Molly laughed. "No, I don't mind. Wine sounds good, thanks."

Solomon was busy opening the wine and Herman was getting the glasses. Solomon poured, and Herman took two and Solomon two. The women accepted their glasses and they clinked them, four glasses meeting, and Solomon said "To friends," to which Deborah quickly added " - old and new." They all drank.

The dinner went fine. The chicken breasts, coated with olive oil, dusted with mixed Italian herbs and bread crumbs, were tasty, the small potatoes with butter and fresh parsley perfect, the romaine salad with tomatoes and green peppers and a few radishes fresh and crisp. Only Deborah knew that Solomon had prepared this entire meal once in rehearsal to make sure he got it right and knew how long things took to cook. There was wine and ice water and drip coffee, the pot turned on so that the coffee was ready just as the meal was ending.

"Well done, Solomon" Deborah said. "Maybe you could teach my intended a thing or two. He's handy with electricity and hammers and pliers and those things, and can fix a flat tire, valuable skills indeed. I'm certainly not complaining, but a little cooking skill would be a nice addition….."

"Women cook. Men hunt, kill wild animal, fix flat tire, kill more animal" said Herman in his best caveman imitation.

Deborah turned to Molly. "The problem is my mother is one great cook. Herman thinks I'm going to produce the same dishes, the same way. I don't think so. What I *do* think is, she has some magic powder somewhere in the kitchen. No matter how I try it just isn't quite the same."

"Could be years of practice, too. You'll probably turn out to be as good as she is. But I know what you mean, my mother makes the best kugel there is. When I tried to write down the recipe it was a small pinch of this and a large pinch of that. I gave up when I asked her how much milk and she told me to add enough so that it was easy to mix."

They talked a while longer, Solomon clearing the table and serving the dessert of raspberry sherbet and small cookies bought from the Hungarian bakery near Consaul Street on the East Side. The conversation continued more than a half hour more, then Molly thanked Solomon for dinner, for the pleasant evening, and told Herman and Deborah how pleased she was to meet them after hearing how much Solomon valued their friendship.

Deborah and Molly shook hands, and Deborah said "I'm so pleased to meet you, too. I look forward to next time."

"Thanks."

Solomon walked Molly to her car. "I'm glad you came. I confess I was a little scared of the challenge, cooking for four. Turned out all right, though."

"You're too modest. It was tasty and well prepared. And I sure do like your friends. They're such fun, the teasing… and they love each other a lot, that's nice to see. This was fun. Thank you."

"Thanks for coming."

He opened her car door, and they kissed. She got in, started the car, drove away. He watched her car down the street and around the corner. Then he climbed the one flight of stairs back to his apartment.

As soon as he came into the living room Deborah put her arms around him, hugged him briefly then stepped back, her hands on his arms, and looked at him. "Oh, Solly, I sure do understand. She's a doll. Pretty, smart, charming..."

"She is, isn't she. So I did this, didn't I? Dinner for four and no smoke from the kitchen."

"You did fine."

"Yeah, my man" said Herman. "I take it all back. She not only really exists, but she is a winner, a prize well worth having. Fortunately for you, the team of Herman and Deborah is at your service, offering excellent advice for only the price of an occasional meal."

CHAPTER THIRTEEN

M olly had been busy, the early school year in full swing, and suddenly Thanksgiving was approaching, time to go to Chicago, the first time she had been there in a long time. The last occasion had been a fun-filled vacation at her parent's house, visiting the neighbors, seeing old friends, giving them time to be with her new husband. Although they had met Darren briefly at the wedding, this was the first time they could sit and talk to him, get to know him, an opportunity to offer a friendly complaint about taking their Molly away to Toledo. Now she was going back to that house, that home, alone. When the school year had begun she had asked off the Wednesday before Thanksgiving, and when it was approved her mother quickly bought a ticket for her. It was a flight in a fancy new plane, a Boeing 377, seventy passengers, that left Willow Run, south of Detroit, 9:17 Wednesday morning to Chicago's Midway Airport then on to Los Angeles. The return flight was not until 5:01 Sunday afternoon, when her mother would reluctantly give up her Mollia.

Monday and Tuesday were rushed, working at the school and cleaning clothes and packing in the evening, then Wednesday leaving home in time to drive to Willow Run, to park and show her ticket and check her baggage and board, soon after the plane roaring down the runway and becoming airborne.

As the plane headed west Molly for the first time felt a sense of regret about doing this, about going home. Going home. Where was her home? And Chicago contained so many memories…. no doubt she would be in her old room, the room with a single bed that she and Darren had insisted would be all right for a few nights, not to worry, and then they spent the nights sleeping crushed together, the first night resisting sex, the second almost forced into it by their closeness, doing it so quietly, so quietly, he moaning into the pillow next to her head. And Molly didn't want to be sympathized over again. The funeral was months ago, Darren gone nearly half a year already, astonishingly quick months, life was going on and she was adjusting. The idea of seeing childhood friends, and their parents, and again hearing all the exclamations of sorrow and regret and encouragement was an emotional gauntlet she would rather not run. Molly regretted not figuring this out sooner, but she pledged to herself to talk to her mother as soon as possible, to ask Mom to spread the word ahead of her. Spread the word that people should be friends, not mourners. Soon the low-pitched drumming hum coaxed her into a brief nap, and when she awoke the plane was beginning its descent.

Molly assumed her mother would pick her up alone, her father no doubt getting the clothing store ready for the Thanksgiving sale. He would allow himself dinner but would be sure to be asleep early so he could get up by five and work until nine on Friday and again on Saturday. Molly could guess how the conversation had gone, she had heard many versions of it growing up. "Like a dog you work, you'll die of a heart attack, what do I need that for?" his wife would tell him. "To bad you aren't orthodox so at least you'd sit in the shul on Saturday instead of schlepping all day."

"It's a big weekend, Friday, Saturday, big weekend, what are you hollering, Sunday I'll stay home."

"You'll maybe spend some time with our daughter? Sunday you'll be exhausted, sleep all day."

"What, of course I'll spend time with our daughter. Thanksgiving, and Sunday, I'll take a little nap, that's all, we'll both take her to the airport. And you could bring her to the store, she can pick out something nice."

Molly was right, her mother was waiting just inside the small waiting area when Molly climbed the stairs from the tarmac where the plane had parked. Molly gave herself up to the joyous hugs and kisses, and then arm-in-arm they headed for the baggage area.

"I am so happy to have you home. I got your father to promise not to work past five, which means he'll only work till six, so then we have dinner. Tomorrow is Thanksgiving, such a Thanksgiving we will have."

"I'm happy to be home too, Mom. I'm looking forward to sitting and talking and just enjoying your cooking."

They had walked out of Midway, located a taxi stand and approached the first in line. After Molly's bags were put in the trunk and they were on their way Ruth Polsky asked "So how goes the job?"

"Real good, Ma, it's a great job, but I don't make much, and I really can't expect to make a lot more with just a high school diploma and the few college courses I've taken. So I'm really thinking about going back to college. Part-time, nights of course, maybe cram in nine hours or so in the summer, but I can be student teaching in about three years, a teacher in four, starting salary then should be about three thousand. So I'm thinking about that. I also think about being a secretary in a bank or insurance company... but now I'm off most of the summer, like the teachers, and when Darren was alive.... Well, it was nice, he could take off some days... So I'm looking at different career choices - not sure which way to go."

"You don't have to decide now."

"But I sort of want to. I mean, no, you're right, not now, not this week, but by the end of the school year I plan to decide on staying a school secretary, or a business secretary….like I said, work all year, but not so hectic, not on my feet as many hours as I am now… or go back to school, be a teacher."

"If you do, elementary?"

"Oh, sure, third or fourth grade."

"Nu, then you'll let me know."

Molly laughed. "Mom, you'll know minutes after I do. So is there anything to eat at home or should we stop at a deli?"

"Shaa, listen to you. We got plenty, don't you worry." Arriving home, the familiar rooms, the familiar carpet, stairs, her old room, hardly changed since her days growing up there. Not at all changed from the nights she and Darren spent in that one-person bed on their last visit. Unpacking, washing her face, reaching automatically for the mild face soap she shared with her mother, Molly knew so certainly that her decision to stay in Toledo had been the right one. She couldn't come home to this house, couldn't go back to being single in this house and what, going out on dates? Having her mother and father approve? Far too late, she was way past that, already a wife and a widow. And coming back to find a new apartment and a new job, to start over again - no, she had made the right decision.

They didn't have to go to a deli, the deli had come to them. Molly came downstairs to a spread of herring in wine sauce, nova, onions, tomatoes, bib lettuce, cream cheese, cottage cheese, orange juice, coffee. And sesame, pumpernickel, and plain bagels.

She went into the kitchen and put her arms around her mother, hugged her hard. "Mom, oh Mom, I love you. What a feast! You're going to eat with me, aren't you?"

"Maybe a bite." They both laughed at that.

Back in the dining room they fixed their plates and began to eat. Ruth smiled at Molly. "So how about I ask you one time, I promise one time, no more. Is a deal?"

"Tell you what, I'll guess at what you want to ask me. If I get it wrong you still have a question coming. Is a deal?"

"Is such a deal, my educated daughter. Look how you make fun of your old mother."

"Mom, no, I wasn't…. I'm sorry, I love the way you talk. We're losing that, you know. All the people my age, we know a word or two of Yiddish, can do some of that Eastern European style of talking, but most of us are becoming just vanilla Americans, just sound like everyone else in the midwest."

"So read my mind already."

"The answer - my goodness this is such good nova, so fresh - OK, the answer is I still like my job, I still like Toledo, I miss you and Dad and sometimes I miss being here, but for now it's the right decision, the right thing for me to do."

Her mother was busy with the herring, looking down, not looking into Molly's eyes. "So, maybe someday you'll start over?"

"You mean get married again?"

Ruth raised her face and Molly saw the tears in her eyes as she nodded yes. "Oy, Mollia, such a fine young man you married, I will never forget that night you called. But you will, won't you - start over?"

"I love you so much, Ma, but I don't want to talk about this, I just… but that didn't come out right. Let me start over. Yes. Yes, I have no doubt I'll get married again some day. But I just don't want to talk about it, don't want to think about it or wrestle it around, it's just too tiring. But today I'm not married, but in… oh, I don't know… some day I will be married. So I get married next year, or in two, or three."

"So no more we talk about this. But someday yes. I like that answer."

"Tell you the truth, I do too."

**

Thursday morning Molly woke early, had breakfast, took a shower and got dressed. She returned downstairs, walked into the kitchen and looked around. "Mom, what can I do to help - and what's all this food for? Isn't it just six, you and me and Dad, Leonard, Rachel and Laurie?"

Ruth Polsky was busy working, her back turned, bent over a square pan being filled with several pounds of home-made stuffing. "No, nine. Such a good thing I bought settings for twelve, although your father said I was a meshuggeneh."

"So who..."

"I also invited a friend of yours you haven't seen in a while. And his parents."

Molly took a carrot from a bag, the contents of which were intended for a relish tray. "Do I have to guess?" she asked, scrapping the carrot, rinsing it, taking a bite.

"Michael Novick. You remember?"

"Mike Novick? Of course I remember. And I know you remember we dated in high school. Mother...."

"Well they had no one to share Thanksgiving with, all the rest of the family out of town, they couldn't go because Karen, you know, Mike's mother, had foot surgery, can't walk so good for a while. So I invited them." Ruth, still holding a wooden spatula, turned towards Molly. "And besides you and Michael can talk about old times and, guess what, you'll never guess - he's got a new job, in Toledo! He's moving to Toledo, you can tell him all about."

"You know, Mom, this looks an awful lot like you're trying to get us together."

Ruth returned to her chores, scooping stuffing from a large bowl and patting it down firmly in the pan, getting it ready for baking. Her back turned again, she said "What,

I'm not trying to get anyone together. You're old friends, he's moving to Toledo, the family left them alone for Thanksgiving... so you know where the aprons are, you can give me some help?"

Molly walked to her mother, patted her back, kissed her ear. "I love you too. So what do you want me to do?"

For the next several hours the women worked with food. They mixed and tasted and baked and tasted and stewed and tasted and set a beautiful table, wiping soap spots off the water glasses and silverware with the hems of their aprons or with kitchen towels until everything on the table was polished and gleaming. All this while Izzy was careful to be nearby in case something heavy had to be lifted or moved, but since no such situation occurred he was free to read the newspaper, actually catching up on the last few days when he had barely glanced at it. He thought about going to the store for a few hours, just a few more things to do, but he knew from years of marriage that would not be a wise thing to do. So he read. When he got a little bored he wandered into the kitchen and his wife, recognizing the signs, quickly assigned him the task of cleaning the half-bath in the hall so it would be nice for the guests. "And put a candle in there from the hall closet, they burn twelve hours, make it smell all nice. Light it when you're done cleaning." Izzy dutifully completed the chore, made sure the bathroom gleamed like the table setting, lit the candle and escaped upstairs to take a nap.

Dinner was at four. At three-forty-five a perfectly perfect turkey came out of the oven, and moments later, with the smell filling the kitchen and spilling out into the dining and living rooms like a warm greeting, the doorbell rang. Izzy opened the door and greeted Al and Karen Novick with hugs and kisses, Karen moving slowly on crutches, one foot in a cast that went past her ankle, Al with a bottle of wine cradled in each arm. Behind them was their son, Michael.

They came in, Izzy took their coats, and Karen was helped to a soft and comfortable chair.

"How much longer for the cast, Karen?" Izzy asked.

"Six more weeks. It is not fun, let me tell you, but the doctor said the pain I had was from an old fracture, who knows, maybe high school. I thought it was a sprain but it really was slightly broken, a thin crack, and the bones weren't lined up right. He says it went fine, the operation, he says once I start walking without the cast the old pain will be gone. I say what if it's still there? He says it won't be, but if he's wrong he'll only charge me full price. My doctor the comedian."

"So can I fix you a drink, Karen. Al, Michael?"

"In a minute, Izzy. So where is Molly? She should come say hello, I can hardly move."

"Molly is here, Molly is here..." she said, emerging from the kitchen as she untied and removed her apron. She went first to Karen, bent over and gave her a big, long hug. Then a hug for Al. Then she turned to Michael. "Hey, Mike. Been a while."

"Hello, Molly. You look great. How are you?"

She gave him a brief hug. "I'm doing really well, Mike. Just fine... and I understand you're coming to Toledo."

With that brief assurance all were able to skip right past speaking of her loss. Of course the Novicks, like many families in the Chicago area, had written to her, sent sympathy cards, expressed regret at her loss, made donations to various synagogues in Darren's honor. Now they were together again, and what was there to say? But Molly's moving the conversation to focus on the future meant they didn't have to say anything about the past, gave them permission to not pause a moment to recognize her widowhood.

Izzy, Al, and Michael all had whisky, the older men with water, the younger with dry ginger ale. The women had wine. They chatted a bit, small talk, catching up, gentle gossip.

Ruth kept glancing out the window. Suddenly she clapped her hands together and said "Here they are. Here's my little first grade angel." Izzy opened the door as Rachael, Leonard and Laurie were coming up the steps. Ruth sat on a footstool and held out her arms for Laurie, who ran to them and squealed with delight as she was folded in. The sisters hugged long and hard. Rachael's belly was beginning to gently round with her second child, and after hugging her Molly stepped back and gave her Rachael a gentle pat there.

"Things seem to be coming along nicely" she said.

"Yes, and it's going easier than with Laurie, not as sick in the mornings, that's for sure. Guess I'm learning how to do this."

"Yeah, maybe eight, ten kids, sounds about right" said Leonard.

"Ignore him" his wife responded.

Molly gave him a hug. "Hey, Leonard."

"Hey, Molly. Good to see you."

"Still love my sister?"

"Mother of my eight to ten children? With all my heart."

While the Novicks made their greetings and coats and hats were collected Molly turned to Laurie, still held by her grandmother. "Do you remember your Aunt Molly?" The six-year-old nodded shyly, burrowing further into her grandmother's arms.

Rachael responded. "Molly, she's talked for days about seeing you again, keeps pointing to your picture at home. She's just doing this shy thing all of a sudden, hope it ends soon."

"That's fine, we've got all evening. Meanwhile there is dinner to get on the table. Come on, Mom, let's serve these hungry folks." She leaned towards Laurie. "I brought you a new book. Would you let me read it to you after dinner?"

Laurie gave another shy nod, but this time with a smile. Ruth released the child and she ran to her mother, who said "Not right now, sweetie. Mommy needs to sit a minute."

"Go ahead and sit at the table" said Molly "we'll be bringing the meal in minutes." Then Molly and her mother went to the kitchen, returning soon with potatoes and gravy and dressing and cranberry relish and fresh baked rolls, then a second trip for hot and cold vegetables and of course the turkey. Ah, what a beautiful bird was set before Isadore Polsky, the master of the house. He said a prayer of thanks for their bounties and blessings, then took a dinner roll, said the Hamotzi, tore a small piece off the roll and ate it as he passed it to his daughter on his right, she taking some and passing it on around the table.

"Should we do a blessing for the wine, Izzy?" his wife asked. "We've already had a glass."

The master of the house waved his hand in an expansive gesture. "Certainly, certainly. Molly, would you do the honors?"

Isadore and Leonard filled everyone's wine glasses, then all turned towards Molly and smiled, all quietly waiting. For a brief moment Molly froze, she and Darren didn't always say the blessing in their home, and she hadn't had occasion to say it since his death. But the years and years of repetition, of Friday night candles and blessings over the sweet wine, did not let her down. The Hebrew came to her and she spoke it, then again in English, the blessing for the fruit of the vine.

Rachael put some potatoes, turkey, cranberries, and a roll on Laurie's plate, cutting the turkey into small pieces. Laurie said a tiny "Thank you" and began eating. "You're welcome, precious" said her mother. The other adults smiled at the exchange.

"So Mike, Mom said you're moving to Toledo. How come?"

"New job, Molly, I'm going to be the director of special projects for the public library system. I almost looked you up when I was there for an interview, but it turned out to be a long day and then I had to get back."

"Special projects?"

"Yes, mostly two things... looking at possible expansion, sort of a scout out there looking at where branches might be added in future years.... five, ten, even fifteen years out... long range planning, and also fund raising, grant writing, working on special events, you know, auctions and the like, working with volunteers....."

"Sounds like two jobs in one" said Al Novick, ladling more lima beans on his plate.

"Yeah, you know, it's the non-profit world. But I really like library work, pretty sure it's my career. That, or some other large community service organization. So Molly, what can you tell me about Toledo? About all I know is that they're still planning a real airport, a replacement for the little one they have now. I'm assuming there are some Jews there, at least a few."

"Now don't you go insulting my adopted town" Molly said. "Sure, everything is smaller... school district, Jewish community, number of good delicatessens... but there are some nice people, really nice, and it's a lot easier to get around in than Chicago. And a wonderful art museum. And a good library system, which I understand you are willing to work for."

That drew general laughter. "Touché, Molly. I'll not be the big city snob."

Ruth smiled at the exchange. Molly noticed the smile.

The conversation, and the eating, continued. After a while Laurie said "Mommy, I'm done. Can I go play?"

"Sure. Bet you'll want to come back for dessert."

Laurie nodded vigorously as she slipped out of her chair.

Molly turned to her mother. "Where is she going? What does she play with?"

Rachael answered. "You know that chest in their bedroom, use to hold extra blankets? Well, the blankets have moved, I don't know where...."

Izzy spoke up. "A new dresser in the attic. First I shlep it into the house then up two flights of stairs, then I get the blankets, shlep them too." He pushed his hands, palms out, raising his eyebrows. "Not complaining, you should understand."

"Anyway, so Mom goes and stocks the chest with books, dolls, coloring books, crayons, I don't know what all."

Ruth beamed. "Today she'll find also some little cars with people you can take in and out. Who says only boys can have cars?"

The conversation continued, lively, fun. When it was time for dessert Molly volunteered to go for Laurie. "I want to see this treasure chest."

Upstairs was quiet, so Molly walked softly as she approached her parents' bedroom. Stepping through the open door she saw Laurie sitting cross-legged the floor, little cars with little people arrayed around her. She glanced up at her aunt then down at the traffic. Molly sat on the floor close by, her back against the bed.

After a moment, Laurie said "Aunt Molly, can you drive a car?"

"Sure, I drive to work every day."

She kept looking down, moving her cars, passengers coming and going. "Where do you work?"

"I work in a school like you go to, kindergarten up to sixth grade."

"Are you a teacher?"

"No, I'm a school secretary. I help the teachers and the principal."

"Where do people go when they die?"

So unexpected, the words chilled her like a wash of ice water. Laurie kept her head down, hands moving cars and people, while Molly searched quickly for the right answer. "Sometimes you go to services with your mommy and daddy, don't you?"

Laurie nodded, then looked up at her.

"Did you ever hear the rabbi or someone say 'And I shall dwell in the house of the Lord forever?' "

"Yes, I think so."

"Well that's where. In the house of the Lord. But we can't know exactly where that house is... it's like... like a secret, but a good secret. So, are you ready for some pie?"

"Yes, and then you promised to read me a new book."

"We'll take your grandfather's big old chair and sit in it and you can sit on my lap and we will read such a story together."

Laurie popped up, instantly standing as only young children can do. "And does it have pictures?"

"Beautiful pictures. Can we hold hands going downstairs?"

"Are you mad 'cause I asked that? Mommy said don't say things about people dying."

"No, shayna punim, not the least little bit. You can always ask me anything, any time. I promise I will never be mad, OK?"

"OK and I know what shayna punim means."

"What?"

"Beautiful face. You said I have a beautiful face."

"And you do. Now let's feed that beautiful face some of your grandmother's pumpkin pie. And there's apple pie too. And vanilla and chocolate ice cream."

"Will you say it again? Please?"

"Say what?"

"Well the house the Lord forever."

Molly bent down, picked up her niece and hugged her hard, saying the words slowly. "And I shall dwell in the house of the Lord forever."

"I love you Aunt Molly. I wish you lived closer."

Molly put her down, took her hand. "I love you too. And soon you'll be old enough to come to Toledo by yourself, and visit me, and spend some time with me, especially during the summer." They started walking. "You know, you can't swim much in Lake Michigan, it's just too cold most of the year, but the lake near where I live, Lake Erie, gets nice and warm in the summer."

They started down the steps, hand in hand.

"Are there beaches?"

"Lots of beaches, nice clean sand. We'll have such a good time."

This last was said as they approached the dining room.

"What kind of a good time?" asked Leonard.

"Never mind. Just a girl-talk secret."

"Yeah" said Laurie, a serious look on her face. "A girl-talk secret. A good one."

***

The next hour passed with quiet conversation, the full tummies, turkey and wine having their effect. Molly snuggled with Laurie and read her *The Egg Tree*. Too soon it was time for everyone to go home. The first to leave were Rachael and her family, Laurie falling asleep and Rachael feeling uncomfortably full from baby and Thanksgiving in close proximity. They hugged and kissed and promised to work hard at keeping in touch, Molly promising to return when school let out, come to Chicago and celebrate Hanukah. Then the Novicks took their leave. Mike shook her hand, said he'd be in touch as soon as he got settled, his new job starting January second. "Maybe I could see you New

Year's Eve, you could steer us to a good restaurant? Maybe a movie?"

There she was, being asked out on a date, a New Year's date, right in front of her parents, her mother beaming that big smile that said all is right with the world. Molly stood there, hesitated, the room watching her hesitate, then said "Sure, Mike, that'd be fine. And we really didn't get a chance to catch up on the gang, did we? I need some high school gossip."

"I'll be ready, write it down, I'll be able to give you all the AZA and BBG news, who's married, who's making babies.....I'll call you in a few weeks."

"OK. See you then." Molly turned to his parents, gave them hugs, urged Karen to take it easy on her foot. Then they were gone. Her father helped clear the table, did a little more cleaning and then headed off to bed to rest up for the big retail days ahead. Molly and her mother worked side-by-side in the kitchen, wrapping leftovers, cleaning and polishing and putting away until all signs of the eight adults and one Laurie meal had disappeared. The stove and refrigerator given a final wipe-down, the women sighed almost as one.

"That's it, Ma, I'm going to bed. If I can climb the stairs. I hope I have half your energy when I'm your age."

"All day long you work. You think I work all day? I get up and make your father breakfast, I read, I shop a bissel, a little nap....twice a week Maj....so you should be more tired than me. Go, go ahead. I'll sit a minute, look at the newspaper, I didn't get to see it at all today. So Michael Novick, he turned out to be a nice young man, don't you think?"

"I'll have dinner with him new years, I'm not promising to marry him."

Ruth raised her hands, palm out, eyebrows up, exactly as her husband did earlier. "What marry? Did I say marry?"

"Your grandmother was a matchmaker in Poland, right?"

"Go to bed, we'll talk more in the morning."

***

That night the food, the turkey and pies and wine and hot tea all worked to move her quickly towards sleep. As her mind drifted, gently fading, she thought of Laurie, of the dinner…. and as she drifted deeper Darren was there, as always. And Mike, what a surprise, Mike after three…no, four years. And Solomon….

***

Friday morning Molly heard her father stirring shortly after five. She faded in and out of sleep, at one point hearing her mother say "Here, a nice turkey sandwich, don't go all day without eating" and an indistinct response from her father, followed by the front door closing and his car starting. Molly glanced at the clock. Ten past six, and the store wouldn't open until nine. Molly slept another hour, then came downstairs to find her mother in a robe asleep on the couch. Molly went into the kitchen and made some breakfast as quietly as she could.

At one-thirty, rested, fed, showered, and groomed Ruth and Molly descended on Clothes By Isadore, a name selected almost as a joke when the store opened many years ago, a fake touch of elegance. "Better that than Izzy's Place," Isadore would say. The store carried a full line of women's clothes on two floors. Dresses and skirts and cloth coats, belts and scarves and accessories. Underwear discreetly displayed on the second floor, never in the window. In the lower level, never called the basement, were men's clothes and two tailors, sometimes a part-time third. This weekend they would all be working. The company carried almost everything in clothing for people in the working world except shoes, and it was successful in large part due to the unending energy of Isadore Polsky.

When the women arrived the after-Thanksgiving sale was booming, men and women on all three floors, the tailors moving from one station to another, the fitting rooms full almost every moment, the cash registers ringing. When Ruth and Molly came into the store Ruth suggested her daughter take a look at some new clothes for work. As soon as Molly started to browse Ruth walked past the first-floor cash registers and fitting rooms and into the back room which held several desks and chairs and file cabinets, boxes and boxes of clothing stacked along the wall, a few tables and one ancient refrigerator. Next to the refrigerator an electric coffee pot sat on a repeatedly-stained table, with a MAKE SURE THIS IS UNPLUGGED BEFORE YOU GO HOME sign above it. Ruth opened the refrigerator and, as she expected, saw the lunch she had packed for her husband next to the bottles of milk and other beverages, and a few items belonging to other employees who hadn't had their lunch yet or were saving something for later in the day.

Ruth picked up Izzy's lunch and walked with it back to the sales area. She stood just inside the doorway to the hall, where she glared at the back of her husband's head while he waited on someone. Feeling the heat lamp, he turned and saw her there, his lunch in her hand, a scowl on her face. He turned back to the customer, pointed to some clothing on the rack, and with a slight bowing motion turned and walked to his wife.

"Now" she said.

"Ruth, in a bit, we're so busy."

"Now" she said.

"A minute, a minute."

"You ate a tiny breakfast in a rush, it was, what, it was eight hours ago! You want I should be the richest widow in shul? Come eat your sandwich, sell one less dress. So you won't sell the dress and I won't go to Paris this year. Nu?"

Isadore Polsky opened his mouth, shut it, took the brown paper bag and headed towards the back room. The truth was that he was exhausted and so hungry that he had a headache starting, not that he would admit it to his wife. She followed him, watched him get some milk and pour himself a glass, open the bag and take out a sandwich with an inch of turkey, the seeded rye covered with brown mustard and lettuce. There was also a small container of carrot and celery sticks, and a thin wedge of apple pie. Izzy raised the thick sandwich to his mouth, looked sideways at his wife and said "Thank you, sweetheart. I love you too." That got a snort of satisfaction and triumph from Ruth, and then she turned and went to find their daughter.

Molly was looking at some dresses. She had taken one off the rack, a soft, deep red, that would set off her dark hair and eyes. "Pretty" said Ruth as she approached her.

"Yes, but, red? Most of my wardrobe is primary colors, even some blue, but I'm so aware of being a widow.... is red acceptable?"

"It is when you feel comfortable wearing it. If you like it, buy it. One day it will seem right and you'll put it on."

"Mom, that was perfect. What a saleswoman you are."

"What, you think I'm married to that man all these years and don't learn something? But don't tell him, he'll put me in the store."

"And I heard you say buy it. You know Daddy isn't going to let me buy it. He'd like me to take home the whole store, but he won't take my money."

"Mollia, which do you think would give your father more pleasure, huh? To give you something because he's successful and he loves you, or to take your money? Huh?"

Now Molly laughed. "You are a master saleswoman. Listen to you."

They wandered some more, shopping, then were joined by Isadore. "You find something you like?" he asked.

"Sure, Dad. Can I pay for it?"

"Every year we play this game, so the game stays the same. The answer is still no."

"Molly, I'll go get the red dress, you debate who pays with your father."

As Ruth went to retrieve the dress Molly hugged her father and thanked him.

"Molly, the truth is I'm getting ready to sell the store."

"What!"

"Shaa, I haven't told your mother yet. But the store is doing fine I'm pleased to say, business is so good, why not sell when I can get top dollar? I've been looking around some, I know I could help manage, you know, be an assistant manager, help a store that needs someone like me, been in the business over thirty years, tell them what's what. Meanwhile Doris and Carlita, they been with me almost twenty years, they could buy me out with a loan, I get some nice money, put in the bank, work a little, travel with your mother. To tell the truth, I'm getting a little bit tired of this, the hours, the worry. I sell now and I'll have.... we'll have.. money in the bank, we can travel. I'll work thirty, forty hours, enough so I don't make me or your mother crazy, but no more with the six days in the store. And besides, I can play more pinochle and gin rummy, which I'd like to do."

"When?"

"When do I tell Mama or when do I sell?"

"Uh....both."

"For her birthday, in January, I'm taking us on a cruise, she doesn't know yet. On the cruise, looking at the ocean, I'll tell her. Sell it to the girls by maybe May, June the latest."

"That's wonderful."

"Before I talk to Doris and Carlita I have to ask you one more time...."

Molly grabbed her father and hugged him. "No, Pop, I don't want to own or run or work in the store. You sell it and you and Mom go to Israel like you've been talking about for too many years."

Ruth reappeared with the red dress, a lime green one, a dress suit in navy blue and two blouses for the suit. "That's all she wants?" said Isadore.

After the women left, Isodore followed his usual practice whenever he took something for himself or his family. He went to the cash register, thumbed through the tickets from the clothes Molly took and added them in his head. Then he took out his wallet and paid in full, making correct change. You do right by the store, the store does right by you.

***

Flying home, the engines droning as the plane headed east, Molly allowed the thought that had been nagging her to come to the surface. She had no doubt Solomon, Solomon her accountant, was planning on asking her out for New Year's Eve. Now she had gone and accepted a date from an old friend. She remembered one of Darren's expressions for such situations...."a-bool a-sheet-a".... an old friend, indeed. He was at least mildly interested, they had truly liked each other in high school, but then their educations and lives took them in different directions. So he could be, might well be, a suitor. Molly looked out the window at the farmland and just-visible farmhouses, the late fall landscape of middle America, bright colors fading to brown and dull green. "How about that, Darren?" she thought. "How about that, two suitors, and I'm not over you."

CHAPTER FOURTEEN

M olly had flown home on Sunday; she wasn't really ready for the alarm Monday morning. School was the usual busy place, so Monday night she just had dinner and got some clothes ready for the rest of the week and went to bed. Tuesday after the children had left for the day she called Solomon from her school, hoping a bit he had already left for the day, not really looking forward to making the call.

"Hello, Solomon Wohlman speaking."

"Solomon, it's Molly."

"Molly! How are you, how's your family, how was the visit."

"Fine, everything fine, it was so nice, fed and pampered every minute....but I have to... something's happened..."

"Something wrong?"

"No, it's... I don't know, this is maybe presumptuous on my part, but you might have been planning on asking me out for New Year's Eve."

"Yes, sure. Double with Herm and Deb."

"OK, well that's why I'm calling, when I was home an old friend, he's moving here, new job... anyway, he asked me out, and there I was, he asked me in front of my family..... So I thought I'd call you right away so you could find another date."

"Oh. Well... OK, thanks."

"So how was your Thanksgiving?"

"Lots of food, lots of family, maybe my favorite holiday."

"Mine to."

A brief, awkward silence.

"Solomon, I'd like to see you again. And Deb and Herman. How are they?"

"The very engaged couple? Lots of family dynamics at work planning the Moskaivitch and Goldman wedding. I'd like to see you again, too. When?"

"Maybe.. let me… after the first? Early in cold January, OK?"

Not in December, he thought. Oh well. "Sure, maybe dinner and a movie?"

"Yes, and I want to pay. You've taken me out four times, made me dinner…. this time it's my treat."

"Thank you. And with Herm and Deb, right?"

"Right."

They said goodbye and hung up. Solomon paused not a moment. He called Herman.

"G and P, bags, barrels and drums."

"Herman Moskaivitch, please."

"Mr. Moskaivitch is out on a sales call, but I do expect him back before the end of the day. Can I take a message?"

"Yes, please tell him Solomon called. The message is - there is a new player on the field."

"…new player…on…the field. And does he have your number?"

"Yes, thank you."

"Excuse me, but are you his friend Solomon….Solomon, I'm sorry…"

"Wohlman."

"Yes, you're an accountant, right?"

"Yes, a CPA."

"Herman was talking about you. I'm Claire Glassman, bookkeeper and floor sweeper here. Maybe you could help me?"

"How…"

"Me and Herman, that's my husband, his name is Herman too, cute, huh, anyway me and Herman, our kids are grown, we're thinking of selling our house, getting an apartment, do something smart with the money."

"Are you planning on retirement soon?"

"Hey, Irv and Max, they say not till they do, they won't let me, but really... Herman, my husband Herman, he's with the city, electrical maintenance, streetlights mostly, a Jewish electrician, nu? So he retires in seven years, so that's it. Seven years. So if we do sell the house you can tell us what's best, you know, taxes, savings, what to do?"

"Yes, sure. I'd be pleased to. When..."

"Could you come to our house? Would you mind, some evening? We live on Larchmont, near Berdan. Four seventeen Larchmont."

"Next Tuesday? Thursday?"

"Thursday seven? You really don't mind?"

"No, that's fine."

"I'll have some rugallach. Homemade. You like rugallach?"

"For home made rugallach I'd come at three in the morning."

Claire laughed, highly amused. "So you come next Thursday, four seventeen Larchmont, you meet my Herman, we talk. Good. For your Herman, I'll tell him about the new player. Some game, huh?"

"Yes Claire, some game. You could say that for sure. I look forward to meeting you and Herman."

"All right then, Bye."

"Good bye."

"Well" though Solomon "lose a girl, gain a client." Then he tightened his jaw and gave his fist a sharp rap on his desk. "But not without a fight, old friend from Chicago, whoever you are."

***

Herman was delayed on his sales call, did not get the message until the next day. When he called Solomon was out, so they didn't connect until late in the afternoon.

"Solomon Wohl…"

"Someone's moving on Molly? Your Molly?"

"Bet your sweet ass my Molly. Sure hope so."

"None of that hope bullshit. Don't want to hear that word. Try again."

"Gotcha, coach. Home runs only. My sweet Molly, no one else's."

"Much better, limp dick. OK, so who is he, and which knee you gonna break first?"

"Can't go that route, not in the CPA rule book. Don't know, someone from Chicago. He's moving here, like we need him. Asked her when she was full of Thanksgiving turkey, not thinking clearly, no doubt."

"No doubt. Asked her what?"

"New Years Eve. Of all nights, New Years Eve!"

"Why is this night different from all other…."

"So she calls me, to give me time to find another date. Like I want to."

Herman paused. "I don't believe I'm about to say this. Think it's the Deb influence….but I think she called you, gave you early notice because she cares, because she's trying to be nice….good… something…"

"Once more?"

"I know Deb could do this better, but I think she really meant it. She got hooked into going with shlub-from-Chicago, but didn't want you sad, sitting on your accounting ass on the big night. So that means she really cares about you. Works?"

"Yeah, works I guess. I'm sure as hell not giving up because of one date. I'm going to marry that lady, I am. And she's going to marry me."

"Best results that way, I'm told."

"So I should get a date."

"Yes, you get a date. Yes, for New Year's Eve. Yes, we double. Yes, you're a tuchas pain beyond description."

"So who…"

Herman tried to convey that he was both stern and bored. "We both know the answer to that."

"No."

"Yes. Sherri."

"I don't think so. That's over, I haven't talked to her in months."

"Do you trust Deborah with love-life advice?"

"Aside from her picking you, I think she's a smart lady. Sure.. why?"

"Come to dinner tonight. Please. Her mother has gone into cooking overdrive. Irv works in the warehouse, he's on his feet most of the day, burns those calories. Me, I sit in my car, I sit at a customer's. She feeds me like him, I'm bursting. Lots of dishes with eggs in them… I think she's trying to assure grandchildren. So we won't tell her you're coming, you can reduce the portions a bit."

"And then what? Too cold to sit in the back yard."

"We'll sit in the kitchen. Make our excuses, got something to talk about….."

"Oy."

"No, Deb will make it all right. You get there five thirty?"

***

That night, following another sumptuous dinner, Solomon's presence making little difference in the size of the portions, the three young people settled around the kitchen table, too full even for tea. As Herman had predicted Deborah had gotten her parent's indulgence for a short conference away from them. Irv didn't care. His regular after-dinner pattern was a cigar outside, whatever the weather, and a newspaper, the Toledo Blade, in his easy chair, and he didn't need the conversation. Simka wondered but didn't ask. In time, she knew, Deborah would tell her. Maybe years later, but someday.

In the kitchen Deborah got things going. "OK boys, why the kitchen conference?"

"Some guy from Chicago Molly knew from the old days. Sees her when she's home for Thanksgiving, says he's moving here, asks her for New Year's. She says yes. Our pal's got the blues."

"Oh, I'm sorry…"

"No, well, thanks Deb, but I'm OK. See the thing is, she called me, said she wanted me to know early so I could get another date. This guy" he said, pointing his thumb at Herman "says it shows she cares, didn't want me sitting home, something like that. So whatcha think? Is he catching sensitivity from you?"

Deborah turned, looked at Herman, nodded approvingly. "This is a verrrrrry positive sign. Yes it is." Then she looked again at Solomon. "Sure, if she didn't care she'd wait until you called and just tell you then. Deborah's advice is to think of it as just a night, let it go, keep asking her out and showing her what a charmer you are. Plus you've got us, your cheerleading squad. He's here alone. No contest. So give yourself a ten-second pout and then figure out where you're going to take her in early January."

"Actually she said she wanted to see me again, wanted to see the two of you. I suggested dinner and a movie, and she said yes, she'd pay."

Deborah leaned way back in her chair. "She said what! Why are we having this meeting? Look, she got trapped into a date with the family friend or something, but she let you know early and said by the way can she take you to dinner and a movie? The lady likes you, everything is cool. Just maintain, steady on as the Brits say, you know? So when is this date? Going to dazzle her before the big night, make her regret all the more?"

"No, she said... after the first. I sensed, just a guess, but I sensed she needed a little room, things might be going too fast."

"Splendid! You men both get top grades for sensitivity today."

Herman beamed. "See, I told you Deborah would make it all right, didn't I?"

"Never doubted it, Herm, but there is one more question."

"Ahhhh, the Sherri question" Herman said, in a poorly done Chinese accent, the influence of Charlie Chan movies on late-night television.

"What?" Deborah said, looking back and forth at them.

"Herm thinks I should ask Sherri out for New Year's Eve. I said I don't want to start that again, not interested. Two reasons. First, because I'm not interested. Second, because I really lots want to be with someone else."

"Solomon Wohlman, this is the first time I have ever heard you too full of yourself. Just ask her out. We'll go out, we'll go to the Hillcrest, somewhere like that, dance till we're exhausted, you take her home and give her a tiny kiss."

"You don't go in her apartment, no matter how much she begs." said Herman.

The other two ignored him. "Solly, it's just a night, just a date. Let her go out with the Chicagonik, she'll appreciate you more. Enough kitchen conspiracy?"

"Enough."

"Enough."

CHAPTER FIFTEEN

Solomon called Sherri Stein the next day, wanting to put the plan in motion. Get the date, go out new years, enjoy, then start again January second wooing Molly.

"Hello?"

"Hi Sherri, this is Solomon. How are you?"

A definite pause. "I'm fine, Solomon Wohlman. Didn't think I'd ever hear from you again. What's up?"

"Well, I thought maybe we could go out again. New Year's Eve, in fact. Would you like to go dance in the new year with me and Herman and Deb? They're engaged, did you know that?"

"What are you up to, Sol? New Year's Eve is for your best girl, and we fizzled out, I mean, when did we go out last, four, five months ago? Thought you lost interest. Come on, cut the crap, why are you calling?"

"I'm calling because we had great dates and New Year's is coming up and I thought we could have a good time." "All true" he said inside his head.

"But we fizzled, right? I mean, you haven't called in a long time, and I didn't call you...I think we both knew it was dead."

He didn't say anything, not sure what the proper response was.

"Tell me something, true, OK?"

"Sure."

"Promise?"

"Promise.

"I wasn't your first choice, right?"

"You were my second." He said it with as witty a voice as possible, and waited, half expecting her to slam the phone down. Instead, after a pause, she chuckled.

"Well, Solomon, here's the deal. I don't think it fizzled, I think you dumped me, or....or.... what's a good accounting term... wrote me off? But hey, I don't have a date, and you can dance, so why not. But if you call me by her name I'll take a cab home right then, and you can pay for it."

Now Solomon chuckled. "Thank you, I will call you only Sherri, and dance every dance you desire, though my feet may bleed. I'll call you, let me know what time, maybe dinner, maybe we'll go to dinner and dance at the Hillcrest."

"I'd like that."

"So I'll call you again about a week before, tell you what time I'll pick you up, but I'm guessing about seven."

`"I noticed you didn't suggest we get together between now and then."

"Oh... I...."

"Never mind. Second choice, I get it. That's fine, kiddo. Bye."

"Good-bye."

***

The closer it got to New Year's Eve the less comfortable Molly was. Michael Novick had called a few times since moving to Toledo, pleasant conversations, but when he started talking about where they should go and what time he should pick her up it felt wrong. She just wasn't excited about the prospect. She felt as if she had two better choices, one was to stay home, to drink some wine and toast Darren's pictures and fall asleep early, actually an attractive choice. The other was to be with Solomon Wohlman. He was a good man, interested in her, the dinner in his apartment had been so pleasant, and she really liked his friends, Herman and Deborah. Their love for each other, their wit,   were wonderful. Molly looked forward to seeing them again, and thought she and Deborah might become good friends. Since Molly hadn't grown up in Toledo she didn't have long-time, solid good friends, and she felt that Deborah might become one, they had clicked so well that night. Not that Mike wasn't a good man too, but they hadn't gone anywhere with their late-teens romance, and no doubt as soon as he got connected to the Jewish community in Toledo he would drift away, not call again. And that would be fine. Meanwhile she was locked into spending the big evening with him. Canceling the date wasn't at all an option. She wasn't raised that way, it would be outrageously impolite. And besides, if she cancelled she suspected her mother would be phoning her within hours, asking her what's wrong. Michael to Karen to Ruth to Molly. So she would be, as her father liked to say, of good cheer. She would go on the date and wish him a happy new year and the next day would be another day. She shook her head; another of her father's favorite sayings "...and whatever happens, tomorrow will be another day." Our parents' wisdom.

***

New Year's Eve, in just a few hours 1951 would arrive. The Hillcrest Hotel ballroom was packed, the dance floor rimmed with round tables that held eight place settings on white tablecloths. Dinner was served at eight o'clock, which included a choice of steak, fish, or chicken, and inexpensive but acceptable Champaign. Dancing to music was from nine until one, and in an extraordinary coup the Hillcrest had booked the Stan Kenton Orchestra.

Solomon had insisted that he drive, telling Herman that he didn't want to be in the back seat with Sherri.

"What, you're afraid she'll attack you when we're not looking?"

"OK, here's what it is. She knows that she's not my first choice. I'm going with her for my reasons, and she's going with me for her reasons, and our reasons, I reason, don't match. So no back seat nothing... we go, we dance, I treat her like a gentleman, I walk her to the door, all is well with the world."

"Such a fine speech. Such a schmuck. She knows she's not your first choice? With what wisdom and smoothness did you impart that information to your date?"

"You... it... I can't explain. Try this. I don't talk to her for months, then out of the blue ask her for the big night. She figured someone dumped me or something, I don't know, she just said it. She asked if she was second choice, what should I have done, lie to her?"

"No, because that would be the first time a man ever lied to a woman. Dick-head, of course you lie to her, dick-head."

"Hey, dick-head, she asked me, I told her, she laughed...well, sort of laughed, then she said yes. So we go out and everyone knows what the deal is. Or isn't."

"So you won't be getting any."

"I won't be trying to get any. That's why I'm driving."

New Year's Eve was cold, about 20 degrees as the sun set. When Solomon got to Sherri's door she already had her coat on, a good cloth coat, dark blue, a contrast with the red shoes she wore. Her light brown hair had been swept up, looking quite attractive. He told her so.

"Why thank you, Solomon. Glad you noticed, you just made the cost of the beauty parlor worth it. Now let's go bring the new year in right."

She picked up her tiny purse, slipped on dark gloves and walked outside, turning and locking the door after her. They drove to Deborah's house, and would have gone in, but Herman and Deborah came out of the door as they pulled into the driveway. Herman helped Deborah in, then walked around to the other side.

"Hi, Deb."

"Hello, Sherri. Happy new year. How are you?"

"I'm real fine." She turned sideways in her seat as Solomon backed out of the driveway. "Hey, Herman. Happy new year. I understand you two are engaged. That's spectacular. Congratulations and mazel tov.

"Thank you" said Herman and Deborah, almost together.

"Date set yet?"

Deborah answered. "Yes, twentieth of May."

"Beautiful time of the year. Everything set, caterers, photographer....?"

"Mostly. Few things to take care of...."

"Yeah" said Herman. "Lots of details to this wedding business. I'm thinking I don't want to go through this more than a couple of times."

"Is he sweet or what? Please don't laugh, it only encourages him."

They drove to the hotel. Inside it was warm, the ballroom filling with people from eighteen to eighty, most of the men in suits but a few in tuxedos, the women all done in fine fashion, their hair, makeup, perfume, dresses, handbags, shoes carefully assembled. At the coatroom in the lobby Sherri took off her coat and for the first time Solomon saw her dress, cut low in the front and lower in the back, her breasts cupped and held up high, the material a shimmering red, the total effect rather spectacular. Herman noticed too, and as he helped Deborah remove her coat, her backed turned, Herman gave Solomon a quick look of offended shock, his eyebrows down. Deborah turned, saw her, and kept an absolutely straight face.

***

Mike Novick picked up Molly Manion right on time. Molly had made the effort to assemble a little party, people for Mike to meet and a distraction as well so she wouldn't feel the pressure to be entertaining all evening. The others were teachers, one Jewish, two who were not, but all good friends from the elementary school, and the three quickly agreed to talk their husbands into a night at the Commodore Perry Hotel, dancing in the new year. Since the three teachers had worked together for several years their husbands had met several times at staff Christmas parties and school year-end and Fourth of July parties. On the way to the hotel Mike and Molly talked about their families, caught up on news since Thanksgiving, and Mike shared some gossip about their high school friends.

So it was a party of eight, the women knowing each other well and excited about getting together away from work, the men barely casual acquaintances but going along with it; this seemed a pleasant way to celebrate and welcome the new year in, and it pleased their wives. Might as well eat and drink and dance and make the wife happy. They all made an effort to include Mike in their conversations, to ask him about his new job and relate their experiences with the Toledo library system; telling of going for Story Hour as small children, getting their own library card, discovering long-overdue books on their shelves at home. The music made it difficult for a conversation to include more than two people, but after the dinner various members of the four couples got up to dance, and others would slide into chairs near Mike and Molly and talk to him, or both of them. And of course Mike and Molly danced together, danced well, had some laughs. And he danced with each of the teachers.

***

At the Hillcrest, the four were seated with another party of four that they didn't know, introductions were made and quickly forgotten. Each person had, immediately behind their place setting, a party hat with an elastic chin string, either a shrill paper horn or rolled-up paper whistle that rolled out straight when blown, and a small paper bag with confetti and steamers. Some had already been opened and thrown on shoulders, but most people were saving theirs until the magic moment.

Dinner was served not long after they arrived, the waiters moving through the crowd, covered trays held high, setting up stands and handing out crisp salads on chilled plates. Solomon gave each of them small colored pieces of paper which indicated the dinner choices he had reported when making the reservations. The paper strips were included with the admission tickets when he paid for them; red for steak, blue for chicken, beige for fish, each with HAPPY NEW YEAR'S EVE YOUR HOSTS, THE HILLCREST printed on them. The males had steak, Deborah fish, Sherri chicken. It was a fine meal, served to the hundreds there smoothly and efficiently so that everyone had dinner before eight-thirty. During the meal they chatted, occasionally exchanging comments with their four table-mates. At eight forty-five the band started arriving, quickly taking their chairs and tuning their instruments, placing sheets on the crisp white music stands so that the band was ready to play in fifteen minutes. Moments after nine Stan Kenton walked out on stage, looked briefly at the audience, turned to his musicians and gave one short, sharp gesture, at which they jumped perfectly together into *Artistry In Rhythm*.

Soon after they began playing Deborah and Sherri communicated, in a manner undetected by their dates, that it was time to visit the ladies' room, and they rose together, the men standing with them. As they walked away Herman moved down one seat to be next to Solomon. Solomon ignored him, determined not to be his straight man. After a long moment, neither speaking, Herman said "Can I dance with Sherri? I can't quite see her nipples, but maybe if I hold her just right..."

"Good. Very good. Tell you what, Herm old chum, I'm not sure of the etiquette here, so how about I ask your date when she returns? What's her name... Deb something? I'll ask her if you can look at my date's nipples."

"You sure you don't want me to drive home? You get sleepy you could rest your sweet little head on those fluffy pillows."

"We are here to have fun, eat, drink, dance, drink a bit more, then head home, safe and mostly sober. Then I will return to other pursuits...no, to one pursuit....."

Another long moment passed, the men waiting, the band kicking hard into *That Old Black Magic*. The orchestra had a singer, a skinny blond in a low-cut dress of black crepe covered in sequins that sparkled from her bright spotlight. They would be playing songs from the twenties, thirties, but mostly the forties, songs especially meaningful to those who served in World War II. Solomon and Herman had just missed the war, but Solomon did serve two years right after college, keeping books for the Army at Fort Knox. Herman had left college after a year and a half, and to avoid being drafted had enlisted, also in the Army, and ended up being stationed only a few hours south, at the Defense Contract Supply Center in Columbus, where he also stayed for two years, making corporal and learning a lot about shipping, trucking, logistics.

The orchestra played a Kenton-flavored *Caldonia*. In the center of the room, high against the ceiling, a large mirrored ball had started turning when the band started to play, and it sprayed little spots of light on the floor and tables and dancers and couples.

"OK, boys, rise and shine. Time to dance with the ladies."

Solomon and Herman turned and looked at Deborah and Sherri, standing there smiling, each tapping a right foot in time to the music. Great music, of course *Eager Beaver* and the astonishing *The Peanut Vendor*, the brass notes almost visible.

***

At midnight Mike and Molly kissed, a quick peck, gave each other a hug, then turned to the others. The women kissed their husbands and hugged everyone, the men shook hands with each other. By twelve-thirty one of the couples was starting to go; they had promised their babysitter they would be home by one. Molly asked Mike if he wouldn't mind leaving soon, too, and they agreed on one more dance. Then they made their goodbyes to the remaining couples and he drove her home. At her door she thanked him, gave him a hug and a kiss next to his ear.

***

At the Hillcrest the evening went well. There were some other friends that they met on the dance floor, and the four spent a fine evening wandering the tables, dancing with their dates and occasionally switching partners. At twelve they kissed, Solomon and Sherri politely, Herman and Deborah with far greater fervor. The band played *Auld Lang Syne*. The band played with energy and enthusiasm until just past one, ending with *Till The End Of Time*. More than half the crowd stayed until the end, the couples hugging, hanging onto each other.

Solomon went out and started the car so it would warm a bit. Once they were all safely inside he drove over to Monroe Street and began heading towards Sherri's home. As soon as Sherri realized she was being dropped off first she turned her head just a bit and looked at him sideways, then back at the road ahead, giving a tiny shrug, perceptible only to herself. When he walked her to the door she moved into him and they kissed, standing there in the cold. "Can I ask something of you, Solomon?"

"Sure, what's that?"

"If your first choice doesn't work out, if she's not.... well, don't forget me, OK?"

"I'm sorry, I…"

She kissed him quickly. "Not a thing to be sorry for. I'm glad I went with you tonight. I had a great time… I mean that. A really fine, fun evening. You take care, Solomon." And with that she opened the door and went inside.

***

Solomon waited until the fourth to call Molly. New Year's Day plus three, that sounded about right.

"Hello?"

"Hello. It's Solomon, calling to collect on my movie date."

"Well that's fine, I'm glad you called." Her voice was light, happy.

"So who gets to decide what we're seeing?"

"How about the girls decide? Give me Deborah's number, I'll call her."

"Sure… why not. And dinner too?"

"Absolutely dinner too. That was the promise. What are your favorites?"

"Well, I don't know if they're favorites, but Herm and I seem to live on pizza and corned beef and pastrami."

"No salads, no cooked vegetables?"

"Mushrooms on the pizza, tomato sauce too. Plus, to be honest, I really load up on the fruits and vegetables when I eat at my folk's house."

"It may not be pizza this time. Let me talk to Deborah about that too. When?"

"Next weekend, if you want."

They agreed, he gave her Deborah's phone number and then they said goodbye. He was thrilled with the lighthearted banter. Definitely a good sign.

CHAPTER SIXTEEN

M rs. Molly Manion had told her mother-in-law that she planned on waiting until the unveiling of Darren's stone, eleven months, before taking off her rings. But now she was dating, really dating, and it seemed time to put them aside. So on a Wednesday evening Molly sat in her living room. In her lap was a tiny jewelry case, made of fine, inlaid wood, not much larger than a pill box. She opened it and looked at the soft dark blue velvet inside, waiting to hold something precious. After a long moment, without looking down, she moved her right hand to her left and worked the engagement ring back and forth from her ring finger until it came off. She laid it gently, almost reverently, on the velvet. Then she did the same with her wedding band. When both were safely tucked inside she looked at them, touched them once more in a brushing motion with her fingertips, then softly closed the box. Her eyes glistened but she did not cry. Molly drew in a deep, ragged breath and let it out slowly, unevenly. Suddenly she stood up and carried the case into her bedroom. Opening her dresser she moved aside folded slips and panties and bras and came to the letters, the love letters from Darren, tied with a ribbon. She put the case next to the letters and moved the clothing back over them, the letters and case disappearing under cotton and silk. Then she turned to her bed, on which sat two sturdy corrugated boxes with RUSSIAN JEWISH RELIEF EFFORT printed on them in English, Russian, and Yiddish, the latter spelled with Hebrew characters. The lids lay nearby. The boxes were empty, waiting, as the jewelry case had been. Another deep breath, then Molly walked the few steps to the closet and began taking a man's clothes out and carefully folding and packing them in the boxes. Darren's clothes. Now the tears came, softly spilling on the material, then on the box lids as she closed the boxes. By Sunday, when the volunteer from Jewish Family Services came to pick up the boxes, the tears would long ago have dried, leaving just a few faint marks. Suddenly exhausted, Molly moved the boxes off the bed and against the wall, then lay down to rest a moment and fell sound asleep, still clothed, the light shining on her and on the boxes bound for people far, far away.

CHAPTER SEVENTEEN

E arly February, Molly got her first call from Mike Novick since New Year's Eve. He called her, sort of checking in, and she sensed from his attitude that he was fulfilling an obligation, that perhaps—no, quite likely—he was getting a little push from Chicago, so when after a bit of small talk he asked her if she'd be interested in a movie, she said without hesitation that she was seeing someone, would he mind, hope he wasn't offended. His reaction, polite acceptance that was almost a sigh of relief, told her she was right. After they hung up she realized that she meant it, she was seeing someone, and didn't want to see anyone else. "Falling in love, am I?" she said to the empty room.

***

A casual date, a Sunday afternoon, winter not ready to give up in Toledo, but the stores showing spring fashions, flower seeds on racks in the grocery stores. Four young adults going shopping, in small part because they have some items they want to purchase but mostly because they want to spend time together, likely end up eating together, maybe at Jo-Jo's, another pizza and spaghetti favorite, or maybe Rosie's. What to do, what to do, pizza or pastrami?

They wandered through the Sears Roebuck store, looking, chatting. Solomon and Herman walked together, Molly and Deborah following several steps behind. As they passed a series of new spring and summer dresses on racks the women stopped and started seriously shopping while the men moved on, briefly unaware they had been abandoned. The women took a few moments, lifting dresses from the racks, holding them at arm's length, turning them front and back, or holding them against their bodies, observing their reflections in the mirror. Most of the dresses were cotton, mostly under eighteen dollars, although there was a fine Irish linen for twenty-four they both took a moment to admire.

Molly stopped, turned toward Deborah. "You like Solomon, don't you. I mean, really like him as a person, more than just Herman's friend"

"Well, you have to ignore the ink stains... sorry, yes I do like him, very much. I'm an only child, and when Herman introduced us it was like my brother walking into the room. It was... amazing...... the most immediate connection...not boy-girl, not sexual, just...well brother and sister is the best I can do, like a brother and sister who've always gotten along well."

"You know about me, what happened."

"Yes."

It was Molly's conversation, and Deborah let her control it. They resumed shopping, holding dresses up for each other's consideration. Then Molly spoke again, picking up the thread. "My mother would like me to move back to Chicago. She doesn't nag, just the occasional comment.... she keeps hoping. But I can't, don't want the tumult, moving and finding a place and a new employer... and like I told her, I've got friends here, and a place to work...for a while I thought someday I'd move back, but that seems less likely every day. I'm comfortable, and for now I'm going to stay in Toledo and see what happens next."

"Maybe Solomon happens next."

"Maybe. Here I am, missing my husband, and this fine person comes into my life, and..."

Solomon and Herman, having discovered they were alone, had done a bit of looking at ties and cufflinks and shirts, but had come back to retrieve their dates. Deborah shooed them away with an impatient gesture. "Too soon, boys, too soon. We have girl talk to do. Go to the hardware department and buy some left knuckle widgets or something."

Solomon furrowed his brow, said the words slowly, trying to puzzle out the meaning. "Left... knuckle... widgets?"

Herman raised an index finger, the bright idea light going on, showing on his face. "I know, I know, talking about us, their favorite subject. Well, we understand your preoccupation, there are so many fine things to mention, such a long list of our many virtues."

"Actually, I was telling Molly how we had agreed to twin beds with a wide space between them."

"And you will put your very cold feet exactly where?"

Deborah waved again. "Shoo!"

Herman lifted his chin, quite aloof. "We will be in the manly hardware department, looking at lawnmowers and grass seed."

"Actually, to be logical, grass seed then lawnmowers" said Solomon.

"Ever the nudnik accountant."

With that exit line Herman turned and Solomon did too, the men leaving the women to the racks of dresses.

Molly and Deborah resumed looking, somewhat serious about the shopping. Molly held up a dress, turned, swished the skirt. "Yes?"

Deborah looked, considered. "For you or for me?"

"Me, I thought."

"Oh yes, I agree, your colors. Wrong for me. What were we saying before the boys showed up?"

"Far too serious words for a relaxed weekend, I'm afraid. Talking about Molly and Solomon." Molly paused, hearing that combination for the first time, slowly repeated the phrase. "Molly and Solomon....."

"Sounds good. Listen Molly, we can talk about this for hours or not at all, or anything in between, strictly your choice. I've never been through what happened to you, or know anyone else who did, so I can't offer much beyond sachel, common sense. Sachel for free anytime you want it."

Molly nodded, then held up the dress she had admired. "I think I'm going to take this one. You're right, my colors. Let's look a bit more." They separated, working at separate racks, Molly with the selected one over her arm, then disappearing into the dressing rooms for a moment. She reappeared and gave the dress to a saleswoman, asking her to hold it while she looked a bit more. She joined Deborah and for a moment they stood side by side, looking at a rack of evening gowns with jackets trimmed in fur collars. Then Molly, not looking at Deborah, spoke from her heart. "I miss Darren, may he rest in peace. I miss his laugh and his touch and his body wrapped around mine. I miss his good, thoughtful advice. Some nights I ache for him so much it chokes me. So now there is Solomon, and I think to myself why couldn't I meet him in another six months, or a year? I like him, pretty sure I could love him. But I don't feel...ready...or am I wallowing in loneliness and self-pity, and I need to get on with my life?" She turned, faced Deborah, only a step away. "How much longer should I grieve? But I can't meet Sol in six months, can I, any more than I can make that car not turn in front of the motorcycle. That happened, and Solomon Wohlman is happening, and here I am."

Deborah's eyes glistened, and she wiped them hard. "Sorry, can't be weepy in front of the boys, turns them to jelly. So I'll say this fast and we'll go look at hardware too. Quick speech. Like you said, it happened, here you are, here he is. I'll tell you this." She paused a moment, considering.

"Yes, I'll tell you this. Solomon is crazy in love with you like I've never seen him with anyone else, not even half close. You want him, you got him, it's that simple. He's a sweetie-pie, and if you say to him that you need more time he will say 'fine' or 'take all the time you need' or something like that. I know my friend, my brother Solomon, and he will pressure you not. Zero pressure. He will wait, sit in a corner and balance his books and wait."

Molly gave her a brief hug. "Thank you. Ready for grass seed?"

"And lawnmowers. And Jewish boys with real husband potential."

***

After pizza, the four were heading home. Solomon was driving, leaving Molly free to listen to the banter in the back seat, and occasionally join in; a three-way conversation that Solomon could stay out of, presenting himself as a careful, attention-paying driver. But in fact his mind was filled with questions, and the overarching question of whether or not to ask them.

It was obvious to him that Molly and Deborah had been having more than a light-hearted discussion of the new summer fashions. He had spent too much time with Deborah, and too much time studying and memorizing and wanting to kiss Molly's face, to miss the signs of something serious just under the smiles. But what was it? And more important, what did it mean for him and his quest?

Solomon thought of the old joke: A boy rushes into his grandparent's house and says "Zayde! Zayde! The Dodgers just won the pennant!" To which his grandfather replies "Nu? Is that good or bad for the Jews?"

Lost in an old joke, in wondering what was going on, Solomon didn't notice a car starting to make a fast left turn in front of him until it was almost too late. As he jammed on the brakes Molly grabbed his leg and said "Darren!"

As soon as she realized what she had said and done, Molly pulled back her hand and said "I'm sorry, Sol." Solomon had braked so hard the car had stalled; after her soft apology it was so quiet. There was silence from the back seat.

"Everybody all right?" Solomon asked.

Reassurances from the back, a barely heard "Yes" from Molly.

Among Deborah's many skills was quickly filling in awkward moments. "Nice reflexes there, chauffeur! Remember to mention this at your annual review."

"I will indeed" Solomon responded, and there was some laughter. The moment passed and they headed home. Except Darren's name was near them, spoken aloud for everyone to hear, and Solomon's leg tingled where her hand had been for that brief moment.

Herman had left his car at Deborah's so Solomon dropped them off there, hearty goodbyes exchanged. As they drove away neither spoke for a while, then Molly said "I really am sorry."

Solomon thought quickly, flipped a coin in his head, and took the gamble. "You don't have anything to apologize for, but if you insist, how about I completely forgive you in trade for you telling me what you and Deb were hatching?" He tried to say it in a flip, cute manner, but didn't quite succeed.

"Sure. Can we go to my apartment, talk there?"

"Of course."

The radio had been off, unwanted competition with the Deborah and Herman show. Molly reached for the knob and turned it. Solomon noticed it, the first time she had ever done so, taking it for a good sign. The music was Gershwin soft — *Someone to Watch Over Me*. The lyrics spoke to them and filled their heads.

When Solomon entered her apartment, he saw but did not focus on the wedding invitation and the wedding pictures in the living room. He had noticed she no longer wore her engagement or wedding rings but had not commented on their removal. What was there to say? So here he was in Molly's apartment, the reminders of her lost love near at hand and in their eyes, and she had grabbed his leg and said "Darren."

Molly got them both some water, invited him to sit on the small brown sofa, sat near him on a footstool. Solomon sipped his water, waited.

"Um, all right, Sol, I'll tell you. I was, I am, trying to figure out what to do about ..... about you and me. I was asking Deb for advice."

Solomon smiled at her. "Well I guess I should relax, shouldn't I? Deb's like a sister to me. She would probably say 'don't write off that accountant,' right?"

Molly smiled. "That's interesting. One of the things she said in our conversation is that she thinks of you as a brother."

"So she said...."

"She said... no, first let me say something about... about my head. Where I am in my life, as much as I can make some sense of it. I'm giving up the past, giving up Darren in steps. I don't wear my rings anymore, but I still have them. And these pictures, and the wedding invitation. I've kept letters he wrote. But I have given away his clothes. Steps. As you know from this afternoon, he still isn't gone. I guess I can't promise that won't happen again."

Solomon had to say it, could not keep the words back. "You love him, and maybe some part of you always will. I do not mind. What matters now is that you are with me, that I am with you. I love you as much as I know how, and I will propose one heartbeat after you say I can."

Molly closed her eyes for a long moment, then opened them, looked down and then directly at him. "I like you so very much. I think it is heading in the love direction. Can you wait? I make no promises, no promises to be able to give up Darren soon enough, no promises to -- Ohh, I can't promise to love you. So what if you wait for me and love me and one day I say I don't love you, it just isn't going to happen?"

"Molly, I'm here. I'm not going anywhere. You take the time you need. Until the answer is 'no' — oy, what I just said — *unless* the answer is no I won't go away. I'm going to keep selling Solomon as hard as Herman sells those barrels. And I'll keep balancing my books."

She smiled at him. "Your sister said almost the same thing just a few hours ago."

"And she was right."

CHAPTER EIGHTEEN

H ard to believe, after all the dating-but-not-proposing, then Deborah going to Florida, then Herman proposing, then waiting for the right date and making plans and arrangements for the flowers and the bridal gown and the caterer and the rabbi and the cantor and the invitations and the candles and the bridesmaid's dresses and the tuxedos for Herman and Solomon and the two ushers and a whole lot more mishegoss that it was here, it was today. Herman Moskaivitch and Deborah Goldman were to be man and wife, married in shul, under the chupa, in hours, only hours. Herman was somewhere beyond nervous. A man with reasonable skills in woodworking and electronics and auto mechanics couldn't get his studs in place on his stiff white shirt, couldn't get his cufflinks to behave. Solomon, fully dressed, only his tuxedo coat waiting on a hanger, helped his friend.

"What are you doing, why are you being such a shmuhk, you've been planning for this day for almost a year, right? Will you please relax. Here, you've got your tie on crooked."

"I can't listen to relaxation lectures right now. I'm too nervous."

"The bride is nervous. The groom is eager."

"You have that quite backwards. Is my hair OK?"

"Go look in the mirror, give it a comb for the thousandth time. Yes, it looks fine. You look fine. You look like you could pass out, but aside from that you look fine."

Molly arrived early. As a friend of both the bride and groom she could have sat on either side. She chose to sit on the left so she could see Solomon's face, not his back. Molly watched the two ushers escorting family members down the aisle. In a moment down the aisle came the maid of honor, a life-long friend, and Deborah's two cousins as bridesmaids, escorted by the ushers, Herman and Solomon appearing from a side door. The rabbi and cantor came from another door. Then all assembled and the maid of honor and bridesmaids and ushers and Solomon and Herman, happy lightheaded Herman, turned to look at his beautiful, joyous bride, linked arm-in-arm to her proud father.

***

And then there was a moment, a bit later in the service. The rabbi was leaning forward, speaking quietly, privately, to the bride and groom. Solomon took that moment to turn and look over his shoulder, to steal a glance at Molly. To his great pleasure she was looking right at him, smiling bright and clear. They were married six months later, but at that moment, when their eyes met, their souls were joined forever.

The End